THE CEO'S ASSISTANT

IONA ROSE

AUTHOR'S NOTE

Hey there!

Thank you for choosing my book. I sure hope that you love it. I'd hate to part ways once you're done though. So how about we stay in touch?

My newsletter is a great way to discover more about me and my books. Where you'll find frequent exclusive giveaways, sneak previews of new releases and be first to see new cover reveals.

And as a HUGE thank you for joining, you'll receive a FREE book on me!

With love,

Iona

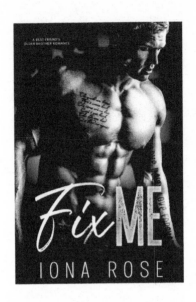

Get Your FREE Book Here:
https://dl.bookfunnel.com/v9yit8b3f7

The CEO's Assistant

Publisher: SomeBooks
ISBN: **9781913990299**

KERRY

"Are you looking forward to the party tonight?" Lisa asks me with an excited smile.

It's obvious she's looking forward to the party tonight, but I'm really not. I shake my head and groan. She frowns at me, her normally smooth forehead wrinkling as she watches me closely as if the reason for me not being excited about the party is going to be written right there on my face.

"Oh come on, why not? You used to be the life and soul of the party, Kerry. You're barely even twenty-six, you're far too young to be over partying," Lisa says.

Am I? I wonder. Because I sure don't feel all that young. Still, age has nothing to do with this. It's more about who I will end up having to make nice with. I'd be much happier if the party was someone else's, or if we were going clubbing instead.

"It's not that," I say with a sigh. "It's the thought of having to be at the same party as Blake."

Blake Colton is the cofounder of Colton and Morgan Co, the real estate firm where I work as a sales manager. My father is the other co-founder, and he is determined to make Blake and I like each other. He's wasting his time though. Big time.

I can't stand Blake.

Absolutely can't.

And I know he feels the exact same way about me.

I've tried to make my father see that Blake and I are perfectly capable of working towards the same goals without liking each other, but my father doesn't see it that way. It would probably be easier if I could just pretend to like him, but that's so hard to do. I'm not very good at pretending. What you see is what you get with me.

The man is so infuriating, I don't think I could keep the act up for long. I can act the part well enough that clients would never know how much I annoying I find him, but my dad would see straight through my act instantly.

"I don't get why you don't like him," Lisa comments, her eyes going dreamy. "He's delicious. Oh, those eyes, that firm, muscular butt… "

I roll my eyes.

"And he's always such a gentleman," she finishes firmly.

"Gentleman? The only reason he seems that way to you and the others is because none of you really have to work with him so you don't see what he's really like. Now why don't I like him? Hmm, let's see. He's arrogant, rude, cocky and full of himself," I cry passionately. "And that's on a good day."

It's Lisa's turn to roll her eyes. Then she looks around to check that my office door is closed. She sees that it is and she turns back to me and giggles.

"Ok, fair enough, you know him better than I do. So maybe the guy's not exactly Prince Charming personality wise. But he can park his Italian shoes under my bed any day. He's freaking hot. Please tell me you see that much."

I shrug. "Sure, he's good to look at, but as soon as he opens his mouth, the illusion is ruined, and unfortunately, he opens his mouth all too often."

Lisa laughs.

"Okay, okay, you win. Keep hating him. How about you just avoid him tonight. It's not like your parents' place isn't big enough for you to not have to get too close to him," she points out. "You can still enjoy the party."

"Normally I would agree with you. But my dad seems to think that Blake and I have to be best buddies or something. And he's not likely to let it go any time soon. I just know he's going to keep trying to force us together at the party," I tell her. "That's what I'm dreading rather than the party itself."

"So smile and pretend like you're getting on great with Blake for five minutes to satisfy your dad and then move on," Lisa suggests reasonably.

"I wish it was that simple," I say shaking my head. "My dad knows me way too well to not see through that one."

"Oh well, you'll have to go with plan B then," she says with a grin and a wink.

"Which is?" I ask, already knowing it's going to be the sort of plan I wish I had never asked about.

"Just get so drunk you don't care who you're talking to," Lisa grins. "And if you're sloppy drunk, maybe your dad will be too worried about what you might say or do to drag you closer to Blake."

I laugh and shake my head. That's not actually the worst plan Lisa has ever come up with.

"Oh don't tempt me," I say, still laughing as I imagine my dad running about panicking about what I might say or do in front of his investors. "Ah it's only one night. It'll be over soon enough."

I check my watch, sigh and get up.

"Sorry to have to cut this short, but I have a meeting with my dad about a new project," I say.

"No worries. I have an open house in a couple of hours and I should be preparing for that anyway."

"Oh, is that one over on Cedar Drive?" I ask as we leave my office.

"Yeah," she answers. "It's a fab house and the area is good, a nice school, plenty of amenities. I reckon it's going to pretty much sell itself."

I nod and smile. It is a great house and Lisa is likely right about it selling itself. We reach the end of the corridor and say our goodbyes, Lisa heading back towards her own office and me heading for the main conference room for the meeting with my father and a couple of investors. And Blake of course. I could have done without having to spend a few hours with him, but at least he'll have to be civil and respectful to me in front of the investors. It's more than he usually manages with me.

I reach the conference room and push the door open and step inside. Blake and my father sit opposite each other at one end of the long table. As always, Blake's insanely good looks assault me. He is tall and muscular, someone who clearly works out. A lot. He has straight dark brown hair and intense, bright green eyes that sparkle when he smiles. Not that he smiles at me very often. Unless of course I count the smug curled-up lip that occasionally happens when he thinks he's scored a point against me.

"Nice of you to join us, Kerry," Blake says, giving me the curled-up lip smile now.

My father glares at him and he shrugs, the smile still on his face.

"What? The investors will be here any minute and we have stuff to discuss. It would have been nice if she'd gotten here a little bit earlier is all I'm saying," Blake says.

"She got here at the time I told her to get here," my father says. "Kerry, sit down please."

I do as he says, sitting a few chairs down from my father and watching Blake who has stopped with the arrogant grin and is instead looking at my father in confusion.

"What's going on?" I say. "I thought the investors weren't due to arrive for another hour."

"You thought that because that's what I told you, because quite frankly, I couldn't tolerate you two spending the next hour arguing with me," he says. "The project the investors are coming to discuss is one that I want you two to work on together."

"No way," I say before my dad is even finished talking.

"Sorry Mark. For once, Kerry and I agree on something," Blake says.

"Look, we need this investment. It can put us in the top earners in the country if we pull this off. But to do that, you two need to work together. Blake, it's half your firm, you should want that," my father says.

"I do want that. And I'm happy to head up the project you're talking about, of course. But Kerry is hardly the only sales manager. I'll choose a different one to work with me on this. Macey has a good record. I'll likely ask her to work on this with me," Blake says.

"Macey does have a good record," my father agrees. "And I'm not knocking her at all. She's good at her job and she gets results. But her team's sales figures are not as good as Kerry's team's sales figures. Kerry is the best person for this, and I'm not about to put the wrong people on a project because both of you have some ridiculous thing going on between you. You're both adults and you will just have to learn to work together. I'm not asking you to become best friends, I'm just saying you will need to be civil to each other. Is that really too much to ask?"

I ignore my dad's question for now and ask one of my own instead of answering him.

"Can't you and I work on it instead of Blake and I?" I ask my father, with pleading eyes.

He shakes his head.

"No. I have enough going on right now and I can't spare the time to oversee this. it needs a lot of attention," he says.

I want to refuse the project, to tell my dad and Blake to use Macey like Blake suggested, but something stops me. The fact of the matter is, I can't really pick and choose my own projects. I have to do as I'm told to an extent. And I don't want to be seen as difficult. Plus, I want this project. I don't see why I should miss out on working on something important just to avoid Blake.

"Ok," I say, forcing myself to smile. "Then I guess Blake and I will just have to work out a way to get past our differences won't we."

"Excellent," my dad says. He turns to Blake. "Blake? What do you say?"

"I say bring in Macey," Blake says.

My dad sighs and shakes his head.

"Look Blake, you know I like to think of us as equal partners in the business, but we both know the truth is that I'm the sixty forty majority shareholder. This is a real opportunity for us and I'm not risking it being ruined because you can't play nice with Kerry."

"Fine," Blake says.

He glares at me like this is somehow my fault. Surely, he doesn't think I planned this? He's the last person I would want to work with.

"Good. Then that's settled then," my dad says, clapping his hands together. "Now, let's present a united front when the investors get here alright? I don't want them suspecting that this arrangement is less than amicable."

BLAKE

I sip from my glass of champagne, smile, and nod at something Pearl is saying about her recent trip to Europe. Pearl is a long-standing client of ours, someone who owns several properties, and is easy to work with. Normally, I'd quite enjoy her company, but tonight, I'm having trouble focusing on what she's saying to me. And I know why.

I don't want to be at this stupid party. Every couple of months, Mark throws some sort of party where he invites our high value clients and other people from the industry plus potential new clients and investors for us to schmooze. It's not my idea of fun at all, but I can hardly refuse to come.

"Would you excuse me a moment Blake?" Pearl says. "I've just spotted Mark's daughter and I really did want to catch up with her."

"Of course," I smile. "Go right ahead."

I hate that I have a reason to be grateful to Kerry, but I do now. She's saved me from having to stand and make small talk for a while at least. I much prefer to stand on the edge of the crowd and people watch. Especially now that these events are mostly pointless.

They made sense in the beginning. Four years ago when I first met Mark and we decided to go into business together, no one knew who we were and having events like this one got our name out there and made people start to take notice of us. Now we are one of the biggest real estate companies in the state and we don't need to do this anymore. We have a waiting list of clients, and investors are clambering over each other to get in on Colton and Morgan Co. I think it's just become a habit for Mark now. A ritual. Maybe he's superstitious and he thinks if he changes the way we do things, it will all come crashing down around us. Maybe it would for some things, like our procedure, but not because we stop throwing parties.

I could put my foot down now I suppose and refuse to come to these things in the future. It wouldn't make any difference whatsoever to the business. But I know Mark would be pissed off, and I like that we work well together and that we get on. I really don't want us to have tension between us, especially over something as stupid as a party three or four times a year. It's bad enough having to work alongside one person I want to strangle without making it two.

I tell myself to suck it up and make an effort and that it's only one night out of my whole life. One night that will be over soon enough. I catch the eye of one of our investors, Thomas. He smiles and comes over to me with his wife Hilary.

"Great party," I murmur in the way of a greeting.

"It sure is," Thomas agrees. "Mark sure knows how to throw a good shindig, doesn't he."

I nod as I look around the ballroom where the party is being held in Mark's manor. The décor is amazing, the food is delicious and the drinks are flowing. Music and laughter fills the air. Thomas is right; Mark sure does know how to throw a party.

"I keep saying we should have a little get together at our place," Hilary smiles. "You know, return the favor if you will. Poor Mark always has to play host. I thought it would be nice to have an event he could just enjoy. But Thomas insists we could never throw a party that would even come close to as good as one of Mark's parties."

"Oh, I don't know. They are top notch, but you have excellent taste Hilary. I'm sure you could put on a damned good party yourself," I say, carefully walking the line between trying not to sound like I don't appreciate the party we're at and making it sound as though I think Hilary could pull off something similar.

"Aww you're too kind," Hilary smiles, her eyes sparkling. "But I'm not sure it's true."

She's pleased with my comments even as she down plays them and I smile and nod.

"Sure, it's true," I tell her.

"Now Blake, don't go putting ideas into my wife's head," Thomas laughs. "Parties are so much better when you're a guest rather than a host. And when she works that one out, it'll be left to me to play host."

We stand and chat for a bit longer, talking about the current property market and an upcoming vacation Thomas and Hilary have planned to Greece. When they finally wander away, I am left alone once more, and this time, I don't feel guilty about it. I've socialized. I've done my part. And now I can take a moment or two to just people watch.

I look around and I spot Kerry on the dance floor with Lisa. I roll my eyes as I watch Kerry twirling and waving her arms around. She's such a poser. I can't stand her. But here's the worst thing about it all. Despite my dislike for Kerry, I can't help but find her attractive to look at.

She's tall but not too tall. Her body is slim and fit looking; she's toned rather than skinny. Her long blonde hair sits in soft looking wavy curls around her face. Her eyes, eyes as blue as the ocean, twinkle as she smiles at Lisa. There's no denying that the woman is a beauty, and tonight, she looks even hotter than usual in her tight red dress and her sky high red heels.

As I watch Kerry move, I find myself getting more and more attracted to her. It's like her movements on the dance floor are drawing me in, making me want her. I can feel my cock starting to harden inside of my pants and I quickly look away from Kerry, hoping no one can see the bulge in my pants.

I turn from Kerry and find myself face to face with Mark. Great. That's just what I need. Mark catching me with a hard on over his daughter dancing.

"You should go and ask her to dance," Mark says, smiling and nodding towards Kerry.

That's good. Not that he wants me to dance with her – that part is bad – but he clearly hasn't noticed my state of arousal or he wouldn't be smiling and trying to send me over to Kerry.

"I don't think so," I say, smiling and shaking my head.

"Come on now Blake," Mark says. "I know you and Kerry are never going to be best friends, but you're going to be working together on our new development and I want to know I can trust you to be near each other without one of you ending up murdered. Or worse, arguing in front of our investors."

"Kerry would tell me to go to hell if I asked her to dance," I point out.

"Of course, she wouldn't." Mark smiles.

Understanding comes over me and I smile too.

"Because you've already given her this speech," I say.

Mark's smile widens and he nods his head.

"I knew there was a reason I went into business with you kid. It must be because of how astute you are," Mark says. He pauses for a moment and then he goes on. "You're right. I did have a very similar conversation with Kerry earlier on and she has agreed to play nicely with you. So if there's no dance, then I know you're the one causing the problems between you."

I think sometimes Mark forgets that we're partners. Maybe it's because I'm only a year older than Kerry and he thinks of me as a kid. I don't know why really. I know it should annoy me and sometimes it does, but mostly, it's easier to just let it go. Mark doesn't act this way in front of clients or other staff members and so I can live with it. And if he's that worried about me dancing with Kerry, then I will do it. But not yet. I need some more Dutch courage first.

"Well as long as you're sure she's not going to think I've lost the plot and run away from me screaming," I smile.

"She definitely won't," Mark confirms.

I force myself to keep smiling.

"Then I will ask her to dance," I say. I hold up my almost empty glass. "But a bit later on I think. After I've had a few more of these. I'm not really much of a dancer you know."

"So I've noticed," Mark laughs. "But seeing you and Kerry dancing together will give the right impression to our clients as well as cementing your working relationship."

I should have known there was more to this than Mark was letting on. A client or two must have picked up on the tension between Kerry and I and mentioned it in passing to Mark or one of the secretaries who passed on the information to him.

I switch my empty glass for a full one as a waiter walks past us with a tray filled with glasses of champagne.

"I can rely on you for this right Blake?" Mark says.

I nod and sip my drink.

"Of course," I say. "I don't plan on getting steaming drunk and embarrassing myself or the company. I just want to be tipsy enough to not care that I've got two left feet that's all."

And to be tipsy enough that I'm more willing to tolerate Kerry I think but don't say. Mark nods and then he excuses himself and begins to circulate around the room once more. I curse myself for ending up in this situation. I should never have come here tonight, and I should have made more of an effort to tell Mark no. That's not what I'm annoyed about though. Not really. I'm annoyed because as much as I dislike Kerry, I can't seem to take my eyes off her as she sways and writhes to the music.

I watch her, trying my best to be subtle about it, hoping that no one has noticed my sudden attraction to Kerry. I really don't want to have to work with Kerry, let alone spend time with her outside of work or start wanting to look at her. She's so annoying – she argues with everything I say, mostly just for the sake of it. And my God the woman can moan. She only gets away with it because she is Mark's daughter and I can't fire her. But still, I can't stop looking at her. She's even hotter than usual tonight, her dress showing her curves off to perfection. I can imagine myself walking up to her and slipping my hands onto her hips, running them over her body.

Jeez Blake, stop that right now, I think to myself, aware that if I keep thinking about touching Kerry like this that I will be hard again in seconds. I seem to have gotten away with that once. I'm not risking it again. No way. But now I'm conscious of having to dance with Kerry. What if it happens then? I tell myself it'll be fine. If I get carried away, I'll just ask her a question and when she answers me, the sound of her voice is sure to kill any desire I am feeling for her.

I grab another glass of champagne from a passing waiter, hoping that not only will it make me brave enough to dance in public, but also that it will stop me being so angry at myself for being unable to take my eyes off Kerry. Of course, it doesn't work that way. Especially as I still can't stop watching her moving, her body stretching and moving all around.

She is dancing with someone else now. Not Lisa. It's a guy. A guy I don't recognize and I feel a spark of jealousy inside of myself. I shake my head. What the fuck is wrong with me? I tell myself I need to stay the hell off of champagne in the future. Why would I be jealous of some guy dancing with Kerry? Being anywhere near her is the last place I should want to be, and really, I should be grateful to the guy. While he's dancing with Kerry, I have a perfect excuse not to go over there and ask her to dance with me. And maybe if she got laid she would chill out a bit and be less annoying in general.

I keep watching Kerry and the mystery man and when the song finishes and he steps away from her with a smile, I drain the last of my champagne and head across the room towards Kerry. I smile when I reach her.

"May I have this dance?" I say.

She smiles and nods her head, but I notice that the smile doesn't reach her eyes. That's just fine with me. It's not like I want us to bond or anything. God, Mark has a lot to answer for here.

I regret choosing this moment to ask Kerry to dance when the next song starts to play and it's a slow and slushy love song. It's too late for me to change my mind now though. I feel as though everyone is watching me. I know that's not true, but it would still look weird if I walked away now.

Kerry really is watching me, looking at me expectantly and I clear my throat and take her into my arms. We sway gently to the music, turning in a small tight circle.

"I didn't think you were going to come up to me," Kerry whispers

"Why not?" I ask.

She shrugs and then she gives a soft laugh.

"I guess I just figured you weren't much of a dancer," she says.

"Ah well, that shows how little you know about me," I say.

What the fucking hell did I say that for? I've made it sound like I love dancing or something.

I have no idea where it even came from, but I've said it now, and she's looking at me expectantly, waiting for me to do something a bit more adventurous than turn her in a little circle now I've implied I am quite the dancer. I have to do something or she's going to know I lied to her and wonder why I would lie about something so pointless. It's actually good timing though, because I can feel my cock hardening again as Kerry gazes at me.

I take a deep breath and then I spin Kerry away from me, catching her wrist and extending my arm and then spinning her back in towards me. I rest my hand on her hip. Her chest heaves as she breathes. She looks me deep in the eye and swallows hard.

I would give anything to kiss her right now and have her kiss me back. I think, judging by the way she's looking at me, she would kiss me back if I kissed her now. But I can't do that. Not here. Not in front of her parents and our staff and clients. I decide to play it cool, to not let Kerry see the effect she's having on me.

I drag my eyes away from hers and spin her again, and then I grab her hips and pull her against me, her back to my front. It's a mistake. Her ass rubs over my cock. I spin her away from me quickly before she can feel the movement deep down in my pants. Luckily for me, the song ends there and I don't have to risk her feeling my hard on. Instead, I smile at Kerry, a cold, indifferent smile.

"Thanks for the dance," I say.

"Anytime," she replies.

She is equally cold, equally indifferent, but beneath it, I can sense something that looks an awful lot like desire. Is it possible that she feels that I am annoying but attractive too? Is it possible she is equally attracted to me? It's unlikely at best and it doesn't matter anyway. It's not like I am ever going to act on this. I am only feeling attracted to Kerry because I've drank too much. I could never actually be with someone as entitled as Kerry is.

All the same, I make my excuses shortly after our dance and slip away into the night. I call a cab from the street and give the driver the address of my apartment building. I get home, shower, brush my teeth and get into bed. And still, I am thinking about the way Kerry felt in my arms. The way her nipples pressed against me. The way the heat of her pussy washed over me, sending goosebumps chasing each other over my skin.

I close my eyes, trying to push the images away and fall asleep, but closing my eyes only seems to make the vision of Kerry in my mind feel more real. I moan softly to myself, feeling more and more frustrated as my cock swells and I imagine Kerry's full red lips wrapping around it, moving up and down my length, her rough tongue caressing me.

That does it.

I reach down and grab my cock in my fist. I begin to move my hand up and down my length, thinking of nothing but Kerry, imagining that it is her hand holding me, her hand pushing me closer and closer to my oncoming climax. I imagine her on top of me, her hips moving, her pussy tight and wet around me.

I move my hand faster and faster and when I come, I do it with Kerry's name on my lips and a vision of her naked body seared into my mind. I lay in the darkness panting for breath, asking myself what just happened. How have I gone from despising her to lying in bed jerking off at the thought of her?

Easy. I blame that dress Kerry was wearing tonight. It should be illegal for anyone to look that damned edible.

KERRY

I glance down at my watch. There's another twenty-six minutes until I am due to go to the conference room and meet with Blake. Less than half an hour. My stomach swirls at the thought of the meeting and I tell myself to stop being so ridiculous. I should be dreading this meeting. In most ways, I am dreading this meeting. I really don't want to have to work closely with Blake on this project or any other for that matter. But despite that, I am excited at the thought of seeing him again. At the thought of being alone with him. At the thought of him taking me in his arms and pressing his body against mine.

I shake my head, shaking away the last bit of that thought, but it's no good. I can't help but keep thinking of us dancing together last night. The way Blake's body would pressed against mine. The way he began to spin me around, moving me away from his body when his cock hardened, hoping I wouldn't notice the effect I was having on him. Oh I noticed alright. And I noticed the effect he was having on me too. The way my skin tingled and my nipples hardened.

The way my pussy felt damp and my clit ached to be touched by him.

My clit is aching to be touched by him now, my body responding to me just thinking about how I felt last night. I can feel my pussy getting wet as I remember the feeling of Blake's large hand on my hip. I imagine that hand moving around my body, pushing my dress up and my panties aside. I imagine Blake's fingers working my clit, making me feel things I have never felt before.

I catch my breath and jump to my feet. I almost run across my office to the door. I lock the door and pull down the small blind that covers the window on the door. I go back to my chair, feeling the heat in my cheeks, the tingling in my body, the insistent throbbing of my clit.

I sit down and open my trousers, pushing my hands inside of them and down into my panties. I can feel the heat coming off my pussy in waves and as I push my fingers between my lips I can feel how wet I am. My fingers find my clit and I moan with relief as I begin to work myself, working off some of the frustration that has built up inside of me.

I move my fingers faster and faster, bucking my hips in time with them, getting more friction rubbing over my clit. My other hand grips the edge of my desk, the knuckles turning white as my climax approaches fast.

I close my eyes and keep working myself, seeing Blake's face floating in front of my eyes. I can almost feel his arms around me, my breasts rubbing across his muscular chest. I feel like I can smell his scent, woody and fresh. I bite down on my bottom lip to keep myself from crying out as I hit my orgasm and it pulses through my body.

My pussy contracts deliciously and I feel a rush of heat on my fingers. I pull them out of my panties and go to the little sink in the corner of my office. I wash my hands, smiling to myself as I rinse away the evidence of my indiscretion. I am still breathing a little raggedly as I button my trousers back up and go back to my desk. I sit down and open my top drawer and pull out a compact mirror.

I wipe a black smudge from underneath my right eye and I fluff my hair up and reapply my lip gloss. I smile at my reflection. I can't believe I have just masturbated at work. I have never done anything like that before and I would have been horrified at the thought of it until now. Now when I think of what I've just done, I smile and tingles flood through my body, reminding me of how good it felt to climax like that.

I try to tell myself that me coming so hard has nothing to do with Blake, but I don't entirely believe that.

Blake. Dammit. My meeting.

I check my watch and breathe a sigh of relief. I still have ten minutes before we're due to meet. I fluff my hair up again, telling myself I'm doing it for me, not so that it looks nice for Blake, and I grab my files and leave my office. As much as I try to convince myself that I don't care what Blake thinks of me, I am still glad I chose the outfit I am wearing now. A pair of black trousers and a red silk fitted blouse that shows off my slim figure nicely. I debate opening a button at my chest and displaying some cleavage but I quickly decide against the idea.

What the hell is wrong with me? I'm a business woman, a sales manager in a big real estate firm, not some ditzy assistant that has to flash her breasts to get ahead. I shake my head, reminding myself that nothing has changed between Blake and I. He's still the same arrogant asshole he has always been. Even when we were dancing, he was aloof, looking at me with a look of indifference on his face, like he could have been dancing with anyone, but instead, he was dancing with me and I should have been grateful to him or something. His hard on told a different story though, but I tell myself not to think about that. Not now I'm about to go into a meeting with Blake.

I push open the conference room door, and steel myself to see Blake, but the conference room is empty. I breathe a sigh of relief, glad that I have arrived first so I can take a moment to get sat down and composed before I have to face Blake.

I sit down and begin to open my files, going back over the figures I have so far and what we need to do to get the ball rolling on this project quickly. I can barely concentrate on the numbers before my mind wanders back to Blake. I console myself with the fact that he'll be here soon and he'll open his mouth and I will remember all of the reasons I dislike him so much and this little blip will be over. That moment can't come soon enough.

I sigh and push the image of Blake away, annoyed at myself for this sudden obsession with the man who I have spent the last few years working here trying to avoid. I force myself to focus on my files. I lose myself in the numbers for a while and when I look up from the file, I realize I have managed to not think of Blake for at least half an hour. Which means that Blake is half an hour late for this meeting.

I check my watch to make sure I haven't exaggerated the time I've been here, but I haven't. Blake is definitely almost half an hour late for our meeting. I pull my cell phone out and open my calendar, making sure I have the right date and time for the meeting. I do. I even check the room to make sure I'm not meant to be in Blake's office or a different conference room. I am definitely in the right place, on the right day, at the right time. So where the hell is Blake?

I close the file in front of me and sigh. I sit tapping my pen against the top of the table, impatient now. I check my watch again. Only two or three minutes have passed since I last looked at it, but I'm done waiting around. I get up, gather up my files and leave the conference room.

I storm along the corridor, heading for Blake's office. By the time I reach his office, I am even more pissed off with him. I am sure he's doing this on purpose, making me wait for him, just trying to show me that his time is somehow more important than mine. Well he can take that attitude and shove it up his ass. His cute ass that looked so good in his pants last night.

Stop it Kerry, I tell myself angrily. You're meant to be pissed off with Blake, ready to give him a piece of your mind, not admiring his behind.

I slam the door to Blake's office open not bothering to knock. It'll serve him right. He shouldn't even be in here anyway; he should be in the conference room. I am slightly thrown when I see that Blake isn't alone in his office. Annette, one of my sales team, is in Blake's office with him. She's leaning over his desk and pointing to something in a file that's open in front of Blake. They both look up when I enter.

"Have you ever heard of knocking?" Blake says.

"Have you ever heard of punctuality?" I fire back.

Annette straightens up and grabs the file from the desk, closing it and pinning it between her arm and her side. She flashes me an awkward looking smile. I force myself to calm down enough to return her smile. Annette is a good realtor, and she's a hard worker. I don't want her to feel like any of my anger is directed at her.

"Is everything ok Annette?" I ask her.

She nods her head.

"Yes, everything's fine now. I just wanted to clarify something about one of our listings," she says.

She turns to Blake.

"Thank you Mr. Colton," she says.

Blake smiles and nods his head and Annette flashes me another quick smile and then she leaves Blake's office and closes the door quietly behind her.

"That was pretty damned unprofessional even for you Kerry," Blake says with a frown. "What if I had a client in here?"

Admittedly, I hadn't considered that possibility and I would have looked crazy barging in here like that if there was a client here, but right now, I am too mad to even acknowledge that Blake is right about that much. Instead I focus on the first thing he said to me. The insult.

"I'm unprofessional?" I say, snorting out a laugh and shaking my head. "That's rich coming from you. I've been waiting in the conference room for you for our meeting, and you're too busy what? Gossiping with Annette?"

Blake shakes his head slowly and sighs loudly.

"Annette came to me because she had a question about a listing like she just told you. She looked for you but you weren't in your office," Blake says.

"Well no. I was in the conference room having my time wasted by you," I snap.

"I wasn't wasting your time. I have just told you that. I was helping one of the team with a problem. If you think that you're too special to wait for a few minutes while I help someone, then you're not someone I want to work with," Blake says.

He keeps his voice low, his tone even, and somehow, that annoys me way more than it would have done to have him yell at me. It makes me feel like I'm being hysterical, overreacting, while Blake is being calm and rational, humoring me.

"I didn't say that and you know for a fact I don't think that. All I'm saying is a call to let me know you were running late would have been nice," I say.

"Ok," Blake says nodding his head. "You're right about that much. I'm sorry. I should have called."

"Thank you," I say, a little taken aback by Blake's apology.

"And?" he says.

"And what?" I frown.

"And it's your turn to apologize," Blake says.

"For what?" I demand.

"For storming in here like a crazy person. For accusing me of gossiping and wasting your time. For being unprofessional in general," Blake says.

He is looking at me with a smirk on his face and I want to reach out and slap that look right off his face. I can't believe that for a time there, I actually found myself attracted to this man. I actually masturbated thinking of him. I shake my head, shaking away that image before it can take hold.

"I'm not going to apologize for calling you out on being late to a meeting," I say. "I'm not the one who was unprofessional."

Blake rolls his eyes.

"Ok. You know what? I have things to do and I'm far too busy to sit around here dealing with your tantrum. So let's just skip the apology and you can tell yourself that you won this one while I tell myself that you're a spoiled little brat. Now, let's talk about the project," Blake says.

I can feel my temper rising and rising and I make a sound of frustration. Blake raises an eyebrow.

"Problem?" he says.

Yes, you, I think but don't say. I have to bite my tongue because I know if I say anything now, I will go too far and end up getting fired. Even being one of the boss's daughter can't save me if I go too far with Blake.

I go to shake my head, but I just can't bring myself to do it. Instead, I find myself nodding.

"Yes, I have a problem," I snap. "You are the problem Blake. You're arrogant and you're irritating and quite honestly,

27

you're the last person in this firm or anywhere in the world, that I would ever want to work with."

Blake laughs softly.

"Well at least we have that in common," he says. "Trust me, this is no picnic for me either. But the good of the firm has to come before our personal differences. You know that right?"

"Of course I know that," I say.

I force myself to walk to his desk and sit down opposite him. He's got me now and he knows it. He's getting under my skin, making me angry, but at the same time, he's being the voice of reason, saying we have to find a way to work together. He's making it look like I'm the problem if we can't make this work.

"Right. Good. So where are we with the project?" Blake asks.

I open the file and pretend to look through it. I already know the information by heart, I just want something to focus on other than Blake's face. Even just looking at him is making me mad right now.

"I've narrowed it down to three prime locations," I say.

"Right," Blake nods. "Why those three places?"

"They're all in desirable areas and they all have a certain sense of charm about them. They need work of course, but we can expect that, and they all fall into a good price range," I say.

"Ok," Blake says. "So run me through the pros and cons of each site."

My head shoots up at that and I look at Blake to see if he's joking. He doesn't look like he is. He's looking at me like he's waiting for me to start talking. I shake my head.

"That's what this meeting is meant to be for. To discuss the pros and cons and make the decision about the place to build the new development," I say.

"So you want me to come up with a pros and cons list for sites I haven't seen when you have been to them all? Come on Kerry. I expect better from you. So instead of worrying about me being late for a meeting with you, why don't you worry instead about having the relevant information when I need it," Blake says.

I can't bite my tongue any longer. I know my job goddammit and I know if I had come in here with a ready prepared list of pros and cons for the three potential development sites, Blake would have complained that he might have had points to add or argue.

I stand up and slam the file closed, scooping it up off the desk.

"You know something Blake? You're just slowing me down with this constant questioning and undermining of me. So how about I just get on and do this myself and you can take a look at the end," I say.

I don't wait for an answer. I leave Blake's office and head to my own, my temper still flaring up inside of me.

BLAKE

K erry has been avoiding me all week. That's a good thing really, because I can't let myself keep feeling this attraction to her. It's unprofessional for one thing, and for another thing, it's totally crazy. I don't even like the woman.

I know I was probably a little bit too harsh on her on Monday when she came into my office after I was late for the meeting. But the thing is, Annette really did come to me for help and I couldn't very well just ignore her. Kerry was right that I should have called her, but it slipped my mind. It just really annoyed me how she seemed to assume that my lateness was because of her. Like I have nothing better to do than plan my day in a way that will make her day the most annoying it can be. It's really not like that at all.

At first, I thought she was right about us not working together. I don't want to work with her any more than she wants to work with me. I would have been more than happy to let her do her half of the work and me do my half and then just present it all together. Unfortunately, it's not going to work like that. There are things that I need her input on and there will be things she needs my input on. There's no getting around it. We need to collaborate on this. Properly. Discuss things face to face.

I get up and leave my office, heading for Kerry's office. I'm done pussy footing around her. She might not like me, but that's ok. She doesn't have to like me. She just has to grow up and learn to work with me regardless of her personal feelings about me. And yes, if I'm being totally honest, then I need to do the same as well.

I reach Kerry's office and put my hand on the door handle, ready to go in without knocking and disrespect her like she disrespected me the other day when she stormed into my office without knocking. I decide against doing that. If we're going to work together anything like successfully, then we need to both move on and start acting like grown ups, and I am going to lead by example. I move my hand from the door handle and tap on the door.

Kerry looks up from her computer screen and she frowns when she sees me through the little window in her door. She beckons for me to come in, covering the frown with a cool smile.

"What can I do for you Blake?" she asks.

She's wearing a blue dress that matches the color of her eyes and I feel myself longing for her touch as I look at her. I clear my throat and look away quickly. I glance back and see Kerry is blushing slightly. Is it possible she was thinking something equally embarrassing about me?

"We need to get to grips on this project," I tell her. "Whether we like it or not, we need each other's input as we go. You need to start acting like an adult and …"

Kerry laughs and then shakes her head. I tail off and frown at her.

"Something funny?" I say with a raised eyebrow.

"Just you saying that I need to act like an adult," she says.

"Well you do," I point out. "Yes, I was late for our meeting. I explained why and I apologized for that. That should have been the end of it, but then you continued to whine and eventually you stormed out of my office like a sulking child."

Kerry opens her mouth to argue with me, but this time, I hold a hand up for silence.

"I'm done arguing with you Kerry. I am your boss and what I say goes. But I am not completely unreasonable, so you have two choices. You can learn to work alongside me, or you can leave the firm," I say.

Kerry's eyes widen for a moment and then she sighs and nods.

"Fine," she says.

"Fine you'll learn to be more personable, or fine you'll leave the firm?" I press her.

"Fine we'll find a way to work together," Kerry replies.

"Good," I smile. I sit down opposite Kerry. "So I've had the site surveys done and I've ruled out one of the sites."

"Which one?" Kerry asks.

"The one over the other side of the river. It's a great spot in theory, but the ground is so damaged by the flooding from a few years ago that it will cost millions to make it safe and stable for building on," I tell her.

"Right," she says, nodding her head. "So we're down to the spot by the park or the spot by the harbor. From those two, I would go with the harbor spot. Market research shows it has a lot more public favor and that people would pay substantially more for a property on the harbor front."

She turns her monitor around and shows me her screen. I read through the lists she has displayed of the pros and cons of the two areas and I'm inclined to agree with her about the harbor location. I nod thoughtfully.

"Yes, that sounds good," I say. "Have the legal team draw up an offer and we'll get the ball rolling on acquiring the land."

Kerry nods and makes a note on a piece of paper in front of her.

"I've made a start on the cost projections too," Kerry says looking back up at me from her paper.

She opens her top desk drawer and pulls out a folder which she pushes across the desk towards me. I open it, impressed that she has gotten so far with the planning already, and I begin to examine the figures she has listed. I tell myself I have to go a bit easier on her. Yes, she is annoying. Yes, she is argumentative. Yes, she moans about everything. But she gets shit done too and she gets it done fast. Much faster than Macey could have.

Maybe she gets shit done too fast I think to myself, frowning a little bit when I spot a mistake in the third column of figures. I reach out and take Kerry's calculator from her desk beside her monitor, entering all of the numbers into it to double check the totals and make sure it is definitely her mistake and not mine. The calculator confirms it. The figures Kerry has produced are wrong. I close the file and sigh.

"What's wrong?" Kerry asks with a frown. "I thought it was quite cheap."

"That's what's wrong," I tell her. "When something seems too good to be true, it's generally because it is. Your figures are wrong."

"Wrong?" Kerry says with a frown. She shakes her head. "I don't think so. I double checked them all twice and nothing was off. And the cost isn't too good to be true. It's only a percentage or two below the national average."

"Bullshit," I say. "Take a proper look at this."

I push the report back across the desk towards her. She opens it and begins to read. I hear her gasp slightly and I know she's spotted her mistake this time. She looks up at me and shakes her head.

"I don't know how that got in there Blake, but that's not the report I put together," she says.

I have to admit that throws me. I was expecting her to get defensive and say we all make mistakes or something similar, but I sure as hell wasn't expecting her to try and deny making the mistake that we can both see in black and white in front of us.

"What?" I say, looking at her with a frown.

"That's not the report I put together," she repeats.

"So where did it come from?" I ask.

"I have no idea," she says, shaking her head.

"And where is the report you did put together?" I ask.

"I have no idea about that either," she says.

"Right," I say. "So you expect me to believe that you put together a report which someone stole for no reason and replaced with a different report, one almost identical, just with the wrong figures in it?"

"I don't know what happened," Kerry said. "And I expect you to believe that much."

"Here's what I believe Kerry. I believe you made a mistake and after your whole speech about doing this without me, you are too embarrassed to admit it," I say.

"You really think I would make a mistake like that? And then try to cover it up?" Kerry says, shaking her head. She's starting to sound angry again. "If for some reason I was going to do that, don't you think I would have at least come up with a better cover story than saying I don't know what happened?"

She kind of has a point there, but I can't see any other way this could have happened except for Kerry making a mistake and trying to cover her tracks.

"I don't know what to think anymore Kerry, so here's what we're going to do. You're going to correct that report, and we'll say no more about it. But I need you to know that trying to lie your way out of a mistake is irresponsible and I won't let it go again. And please, next time you're putting together a report, triple check it. If we had shown that to the board, your incompetence would have made us both look stupid."

"My incompetence?" Kerry repeats. She glares at me and I have never seen her looking so angry. "My incompetence? How dare you?"

"Look…" I start, holding my hands up.

"No," Kerry says. "I don't want to hear anymore from you right now. In fact, I don't even want to look at you."

"Excuse me?" I say, slightly taken aback by her attitude.

"Get out of my office Blake," Kerry says. "I will correct the report and bring the new version to you by the end of the day."

I can hear the anger in her voice and as much as I want to drive home the point that it's not unreasonable for me to expect her not to make such stupid mistakes, I figure now probably isn't the right time for it. I'll let her calm down a bit and then talk to her when she has a better chance of understanding.

"I want the report by two o'clock," I say as I stand up. "And make damned sure it's right this time."

I leave the office without giving her a chance to respond. I go back to my own office, debating what to do next. I have good grounds now to get Kerry thrown off this project. I didn't want to work with her in the first place, and now I could go to Mark and tell him what happened and he would have no choice but to agree with me that Macey is the right person for this now. Yes, her work would be slower, but it would at least be right.

But something stops me as I reach for the phone on my desk. I can't help but picture Kerry in her red dress, her body pressed against mine, the coconut scent of her hair wafting into my nostrils. That version of Kerry is someone I would very much like to spend some more time with. And as much as Kerry gets on my last nerve, I know if I go to Mark with this, he's likely to insist on demoting her and I don't want that.

I don't want to work with her directly, but I know she's damned good at what she does and we'd be crazy to throw that away because of one mistake. The mistake keeps niggling at me though, because Kerry was right. It was such a basic error, and I would have bet my last dollar that Kerry would never have made a mistake like that. But she did. Her explanation wasn't even close to convincing.

I'm going to have to go over everything she produces for this project with a fine tooth comb now. One more stupid mistake like that, and I won't be able to let it go again. This project is far too big and far too important to let myself be swayed in my decisions by how good someone looks in a red dress.

KERRY

I watch the door to my office for a few minutes after Blake has gone through it. I am shaking with anger as I stare at the door. I can't believe the nerve of Blake right now. I have managed to avoid him all week, and then he seeks me out and insults me several times over the half an hour he's in here.

First he implies I'm childish and stupid and then he says that he thinks that not only would I make a mistake that's so obvious a ten year old wouldn't make it, but that I would then try and lie my way out of it with the least sophisticated lie ever. I half wish I had lied. I would have been able to come up with something much more believable than the actual truth.

Because the truth is exactly what I told Blake. That report that he read is not the report I generated. The report I generated was correct. I have no idea where that one went or where the incorrect one came from. I can't even begin to try and work it out. I am too mad to think straight right now.

I turn to my computer and open up the original report. I hit print and double check it is indeed my report this time. It is. I debate holding onto it for now, making Blake wait, but I decide against it. If I take it right now, it will prove my point. He'll have to see that I couldn't possibly have redone the report so quickly. I get up and go to the printer and snatch the report off it. I leave my office, walking so quickly I am almost running, and I go straight to Blake's office with the new report. I tap on the door and wait for him to call out for me to come in and then I open the door. Blake looks surprised to see me.

"Kerry. Is there a problem?" he asks with a frown.

I shake my head as I walk over to Blake's desk and put the report down.

"Nope," I say. "I was just bringing you the correct report like you asked me to."

"But you've barely had five minutes since I left your office. There's no way you can have redone this," Blake says.

"I know," I agree. "I didn't have to redo it. Like I told you, the incorrect report wasn't my report. All I had to do was hit print and bring it to you."

"But..." Blake starts.

"I'll be in my office whenever you're ready to apologize to me," I say with a smile and then I pull the door shut and leave Blake's office.

I go back to my own office and close the door quietly behind me. I lean back against it for a moment and then I go back to my desk and sit down and shake my head, trying to make sense of what happened with the report. I give up. No matter which way I look at it, it doesn't make any sense. I print another copy of the correct report and change it over in my file, looking for any clues as to how the incorrect report got there. There's nothing at all to help me work it out.

It's almost five o'clock when there's a knock on my office door and I resist the urge to grin. Blake has finally accepted that he was in the wrong and has come to apologize to me. I decide to be gracious and accept his apology without making a big deal out of it. I look up and beckon for him to come in, but it's not him. It's Sasha, my assistant.

"I'm off," Sasha says with a smile. "I just wanted to check you had remembered about the conference tomorrow."

I groan and nod. I've been trying my best to forget about the damned thing, but it hasn't worked.

"I have Sasha. Thanks for the reminder though," I smile.

"No worries," she says. "Have a good weekend."

"You too," I reply.

Sasha leaves my office. I know I won't be going to have a good weekend. The conference itself won't be so bad. It's a chance to reconnect with others in the realtor sector, listen to a few speeches and generally network. The food is usually damned good, and the drinks flow constantly. That will all be fine. The part I'm dreading is the fact that I am going with Blake. Normally my dad and I go, but this year, my dad has something else going on and so Blake volunteered to take his place, thinking he would be able to choose who he took with him. It didn't work that way, and I am now fated to spend the weekend with him. And he still hasn't admitted he was wrong about the report or apologized to me. Great. This is going to be some weekend.

I sigh and run my hands over my face. I stand up quickly and grab my hand bag, throwing my things into it. Suddenly, I really want to go to a bar and have a couple of cocktails. And it is Friday after all. I'm already packed for tomorrow, so as long as I don't over do it, it'll be fine.

I hurry to Lisa's office hoping to catch her before she leaves for the day. I am in luck. She's just putting her jacket on when I arrive at her office door.

"We need to go for drinks. Like now," I say.

Lisa laughs and nods her head.

"I thought you would never ask," she says.

She finishes putting her coat on and steps out of her office and closes the door. We head out of the building and start walking towards the nearest bar.

"Rough day?" I ask.

Lisa nods and pulls a face.

"Fucking Darlene from Hobbs and Banks stole one of my listings the bitch," she says.

"No way. I hate that woman," I say.

"Yup. Me too. She has the morals of a fucking sewer rat. Now enough talk about her. What's wrong with you?" Lisa asks me.

I debate telling her everything, but in the end, I decide against it. I am upset about Blake's accusations and his refusal to believe me when I told him I didn't know what had happened, but I know I shouldn't be. It's just his manner and in fairness, until I produced the new report so quickly, my story did sound made up. I can't help being a bit upset about it all the same, but if I tell Lisa about it, she will only tell me I'm overreacting and I know that she's right. I go with the other half of the story instead.

"I have that conference with Blake this weekend," I say.

"Oh that's not so bad," Lisa says.

I raise an eyebrow and she laughs.

"What? I just mean you'll only really have to put up with him on the flight. And that's what? Thirty minutes or so? After that, you can socialise with everyone else and just keep away from him," she says.

I consider this and nod and smile.

"You know what? You're right," I say. "I feel better already."

"Yeah? Well I don't, so we're still having drinks," she laughs.

"Deal," I say, linking my arm through hers and laughing.

We arrive at the pub and go inside. I go to the bar and order two cosmopolitans. Lisa raises an eyebrow when she sees them.

"We're really going for it then," she says.

"Sure. Why not?" I grin.

"There's no reason for me not to have cocktails," Lisa smiles as I sit down and hand her one of the drinks. "But I thought you would want to be taking it easy with the early flight tomorrow."

"Ah I'll be alright," I say, waving away her concern. "I'm only going to have a couple."

I should have known even when I said it that those were famous last words, but in the moment, I really meant it. My plan was to have a few cocktails and then switch to wine or lager. But instead, I ended up sticking on cocktails for far too long, and then moving on to gin and tonic, a bad combination if ever I saw one. And the shots Lisa and I sank really didn't help either. By two am, instead of being tucked up in bed like I should have been, I am dragging Lisa onto the dance floor in a club.

My head is spinning and my balance isn't exactly perfect, but I am having a good time and I am a lot less stressed than I had been this afternoon at the office. Clearly, the night out had been a damned good idea.

Lisa leans in closer to me as we bop around the dance floor and says something. I miss most of it except for one word. Blake.

"Huh?" I say, wondering why she's bringing him up now. It's like she wants to spoil my happy mood or something.

"Blake. At the bar," she repeats.

I look at the bar and I see that she's right. Blake is there. He's sitting on a bar stool sipping from a bottle of beer. He hasn't seen Lisa and I, or if he has, he's doing a good job of pretending that he hasn't. I tell myself it doesn't matter either way, but it does. It's one thing if he hasn't seen us, but if he has seen us and he's just choosing to ignore me, then I think my stress levels would fly up all over again.

I try to ignore that voice in my head, just like I try to ignore how good Blake looks. He's wearing black jeans and a white t-shirt and he looks better than half of the guys in here look in their designer stuff. He is effortlessly hot. As I watch him, a pretty brunette wanders over to Blake. She says something to him and he gives her a half smile and then goes back to his beer. The girl tries again and gets an equally unenthusiastic response. She moves away from Blake.

I try to pull my eyes away from him and concentrate on having a good night. The whole point of tonight was to get drunk, have fun, and forget all about Blake, and yet somehow, here he is, and suddenly, it feels like the night is all about Blake, like it's all been about just leading me to this moment.

I glance back at Blake. Another girl is talking to him, and again, he's pretty standoffish, just sipping his beer and acknowledging her enough to be polite but nowhere near enough to imply he's interested in her. It makes the way he talks to me seem almost warm and fuzzy.

"Why don't you go and talk to him?" Lisa shouts over the thumping music.

"Because I don't want to," I shout back. "He'll only end up pissing me off."

"You mean you're afraid you will let yourself admit that you like him," Lisa says.

"Like him? I can't stand him," I say, shaking my head.

"Oh yeah?" Lisa says with a grin. "Then prove it. Stop looking at him."

"Fine," I laugh.

I keep dancing, forcing myself to not look at Blake. I really want to. I just want to know if he's still at the bar or not and if a girl who he likes the look of has caught his attention yet. I don't look though. I don't want to give Lisa any reason to think I like Blake.

Do I like Blake? Hell no. But do I find him attractive? Hell yes. There's no denying that I do find him attractive. But I could never get Lisa to understand that I can find Blake attractive and still not want anything to happen between us. Why would I want anything to happen with someone I don't like as a person?

"Another round?" Lisa says.

I smile and nod and she begins to work her way through the crowd on the dance floor towards the bar. I watch her go, still dancing, and I realize this is my chance. I can look at the bar now, see if I can spot Blake, and if Lisa catches me, I can say I was looking for her.

I move to the left slightly, giving myself a clear view of the bar area. My heart skips a beat when I spot Blake still sitting in the same place at the bar. He isn't talking to any girls and I can't help but smile. I ask myself why I am bothered either way and I tell myself not to even answer that one. It would just be opening up a huge can of worms. A can of worms I don't want or need opening in my life.

Blake turns and looks out across the dance floor. Maybe he can feel my eyes on him, because he looks straight at me. He doesn't just roam his eyes across me and look away. Instead, he looks me straight in the eye and holds my gaze. I find myself unable to look away from him. It's like his gaze holds me in place. I can't move. I am just standing stock still in the middle of the dance floor and I don't even care. I feel like I can't breathe, although in truth, I am practically panting. I can barely think straight. I can feel my clit tingling, my pussy getting wet just looking into Blake's eyes.

He stands up and starts walking towards me and the movement breaks our eye contact and that breaks the spell he had held me under. I can breathe normally again. I can move again. I can even think again, although all I can think about is the way I want Blake to kiss me, to hold me, to lick me and caress me.

By the time Blake reaches me, I am dancing again, and I have regained my composure. Or at least I have regained enough of my senses to be able to pretend like I have and for now, that will have to be enough. I turn slightly as Blake approaches me so that my back is to him.

I feel a hand on my shoulder. Blake's hand. A shiver of desire goes through me as he leans closer and whispers into my ear, making the skin on my neck start tingling where his breath tickles me.

"Would you like to dance?" he says.

I turn to face him and flash him a quick smile.

"Hey Blake," I say casually, like his gaze hasn't just had me pinned to the spot. "I already am dancing."

"I meant with me," he says.

"No thank you," I say.

He might be hot – ok, there's no might about it; he is hot - but that doesn't mean I am ready to just let go of what happened today.

"That's a shame, because I wanted to apologize for today," Blake says.

I frown, sure I'm walking into a trap or something.

"Really?" I demand.

"Really," Blake says. He reaches down and takes my hand in one of his for a second. Electricity rushes up my arm and across my shoulders. I swallow hard and look down at our joined hands. Blake releases my hand and I look up at his face. "I should have accepted your word Kerry. I know you wouldn't make such a rookie error and I know you wouldn't try to lie your way out of it if you did make a mistake. I'm sorry."

I shrug one shoulder and smile a little bit.

"It's ok," I say, sticking with my plan from earlier to be gracious about his apology.

Blake shakes his head.

"Not yet it's not," he says.

I frown and he grins at me, and before I know what's happening, he grabs me and pulls me against him and starts to dance with me. I don't try to fight him. Instead, I let him lead me around the dance floor, moving my body against his. I don't know what's going on, or why I am suddenly so attracted to Blake, but I know if he kissed me now, I wouldn't try to stop him. Hell, if he tried to fuck me now, I wouldn't try to stop him. I am almost willing him to do it.

I look up at him and he looks back down at me, and for a second, I think we're actually going to kiss. My stomach swirls in anticipation of his lips on mine and my pussy clenches at the thought of Blake's tongue moving into my mouth, rubbing on mine. He starts to move his face down towards mine, but before he can get close enough to kiss me, Lisa is back beside me with two drinks in her hands. Dammit.

Blake steps back from me slightly, and with the almost kiss forgotten, I turn excitedly to Lisa.

"Look. It's Blake," I say.

"Yeah, I know," Lisa laughs.

"Blake. It's Lisa from the office," I say.

"Hey Lisa," Blake says.

He and Lisa share an amused look and I realize they're most likely laughing at me. I am more than a little tipsy but I don't care. I turn back to Blake ready to dance again and then I hiccup and the sound makes me giggle. Blake laughs softly and puts his hand on the small of my back.

"Come on, let's get you sitting down for a while," he says.

I nod and let him lead me off the dance floor to a small table beside it. I sit down a little heavily and Blake sits down beside me. Lisa sits down opposite us.

"Are you ok?" she asks me.

I smile and nod.

"I'm fine. I just have the hiccups," I say.

I hiccup on the word hiccup and Lisa and I both laugh.

"Do you want a glass of water or something?" Blake asks me.

I shake my head and reach for my drink Lisa has bought me.

"No. I want this," I grin.

"Cheers," Lisa says, clinking her glass against mine.

"Cheers," I repeat.

I take a drink of my gin and tonic and hiccup after I swallow which makes Lisa and I laugh again. Blake smiles but he doesn't laugh. Instead, he looks at me with a look of concern. I roll my eyes.

"Will you stop looking at me like that?" I say. "I only have the hiccups."

"Sorry," Blake says. He flashes me a grin. "Just I keep thinking you're going to throw up and these are expensive shoes."

I laugh and shake my head.

"Don't worry about that," Lisa laughs. "She won't part with her alcohol that easily."

"Damned right I won't," I laugh. I turn to Blake. "What are you doing here anyway?"

"I come here most weekends," he says. "There's usually a couple of us but the others have a weekend away booked."

"And you weren't invited," I tease him. "Yeah. I get it."

"I couldn't make it because of the conference," he corrects me with a smile.

"Oh the conference. I forgot about that. We're going to have so much fun," I say. "We can get drunk and dance the night away."

Blake smiles and nods his head. I jump to my feet and grab his hand.

"Come on. Let's dance now. I love this song," I say.

He gets up with me and I turn to Lisa.

"Come on," I say, beckoning to her.

"I'll wait here with the drinks," she grins.

I know what she's doing. She's making herself scarce so that Blake and I can be alone. I would normally have argued with her and dragged her up, but I can't quite bring myself to do it right now. I do kind of want to be alone with Blake for a moment. I want to feel his arms around me as we dance. I want to feel his chest against mine. I want him. Shit. I want him so damned bad.

I lead Blake out onto the dance floor and we begin to dance. I let go of my thoughts, let go of the voice that keeps warning me that doing anything with Blake would be a bad idea. I know it would and I don't intend to let anything happen between us, but surely dancing with him is harmless.

We dance for a while and then Blake takes my hand and nods back towards our table.

"Come on, let's go back for a while. Poor Lisa must think we don't want her around," he says.

Does that mean he doesn't want her around? That he was thinking the same thing as I was? Or is it his way of telling me we're getting a little bit too close and this way he can keep me at arm's length without risking upsetting me? Maybe he just means exactly what he said.

Either way, I allow him to lead me back to the table and I sit back down. I see that Lisa's glass is empty and I stand straight back up.

"It's my round. Same again?" I ask her.

"Actually, I'm going to call it a night if you don't mind," she says, also getting up.

"Aww no, don't go yet," I say.

She steps closer and pulls me into a hug.

"Give Blake a chance," she whispers.

"Is that why you're leaving? Because you think I'm into Blake?" I say, holding her out at arm's length for a moment and studying her face.

She shakes her head.

"No," she says. "I'm leaving because I'm ready for my bed. But you are into Blake, no matter how much you try to deny it."

She's probably right, and the more I try to deny it, the more she'll think she's hit on the truth. Instead of trying to deny it, I go with something that is almost a denial of it, and something that I am certain is the truth.

"Nothing is going to happen between Blake and I," I say.

"We'll see," Lisa says with a mischievous grin. "Now enjoy the rest of your night and I'll see you on Monday."

We hug again.

"Have a good weekend," I say, kissing her on the cheek and then releasing her.

"Is Lisa leaving?" Blake asks.

I turn and nod and grin at him.

"Yup," I say. "So now you have no excuses when you can't keep up with me on the dance floor."

I pick up my glass and drink half of it down in one go and then I hold my hand out to Blake. He takes it and I feel that tingling feeling again as I lead him back onto the dance floor. We dance and dance, and as we move, I am aware of the chemistry between us, the raw sexuality bubbling away beneath the surface and I know in that moment that this sudden attraction isn't one sided. Blake feels it too. I know he does.

I can see it in his eyes when he looks at me. I can feel it in the way he caresses my skin as he holds me as we dance. I am desperate for us to kiss and I decide to drink down the last of my drink and get rid of my glass so I can wrap my arms around Blake and pull his face down to mine for a kiss.

I take a big gulp of my drink and I manage to cough and hiccup at the same time as I try to swallow it which ends up with me spitting it back into the glass. I look at Blake and I giggle and he smiles and shakes his head.

"Come on Kerry," he says, holding his hand out. "Let's get you home."

I nod and take his hand. I knew the attraction I could feel out on the dance floor wasn't one sided. Blake wants to take me home and I am more than open to that idea.

BLAKE

I know by the way Kerry is looking at me that she feels this chemistry between us as strongly as I do. Dancing with her was like slow torture, her being so close to me, our bodies touching, and yet nothing happening between us. We almost kissed, but then the moment between us was broken and we never did find our way back to it. She looked so damned good and more than anything, I wanted to kiss her, fuck her, lick her all over. I wanted to hold her and never let her go. But of course I couldn't do any of that. I shouldn't want to do any of that. I don't even fucking like her.

I can understand why Kerry has chilled out a bit and let her guard down. She's drunk and in that situation, often sense goes out of the window. But why am I feeling this way? I've only had a couple of bottles of beer. Not even enough to be slightly tipsy let alone drunk. And still, I want Kerry. I shouldn't want her. She is still every bit as irritating as she has always been. She is still someone I don't want to be around.

And yet, not only do I find myself becoming more and more physically attracted to her, I also find myself worrying about her safety, hence the reason I offered her a ride home instead of putting her into a cab. I think, judging by the way she looked at me as I led her out of the club, that she thinks my offer is to take her home and accompany her inside. That is not my intention in the least. I do want her; I really do, even though I know I shouldn't. But it doesn't matter how much I want her right now. She's drunk. Like drunk, drunk, and I have no intention of doing anything with anyone that drunk. It would feel too much like I was taking advantage of her.

I smile at Kerry, trying to shift some of the sexual tension that is fizzing between us as I keep my hand on the small of her back to keep her steady on her feet. She returns my smile and then she giggles slightly.

"Where are we going?" she asks. She frowns and looks around as though she's surprised to see we're outside all of a sudden. "I thought we were dancing."

"We were, but the club is closed now," I lie. "I'm going to drive you home, remember."

She ponders this and then she nods her head and smiles at me again, her frown melting away.

"Ok. We can drink and dance and dance and drink when we get to my place," she says.

I have no intention of doing that, but I smile and nod. I don't want to get into a fight with her here. I help her across the parking lot and to my car. I prop her against the passenger side door while I dig my car keys out of my pocket. As I start to pull them out, Kerry grabs my wrist.

"You can't drive. You're drunk," she slurs.

"I think you'll find that's you who is drunk," I smile.

"Oh I'm drunk too," she agrees. "But I'm not planning to drive."

"I'm not drunk," I reassure her. "I've only had two or three small beers."

She ponders this for a moment and then she smiles and releases my wrist.

"Can you give me a ride home then?" she asks.

"Sure," I smile as though that wasn't the plan already.

I have never seen Kerry like this before. I have seen her slightly tipsy at some of Mark's parties, but I've never seen her drunk enough to lose control this way. It's hard not to laugh, but I have a feeling if I do, it'll ruin everything. She'll think I'm being nasty, laughing at her rather than with her, and we'll end up fighting. It's kind of cute watching her this way. She's so innocent seeming; not like the Kerry I know at all. I wish she could be like this all of the time. Ok, maybe not entirely like this, but friendly and smiley.

"Maybe we can even have a drink when we get there," she says. "And a dance too if you want to. I can put some music on for us."

"Maybe," I say, pulling the passenger side door to my car open. I take hold of Kerry around the waist with one arm and lead her towards the door, gesturing for her to get into the car. I put my hand on her head, stopping her from banging it. "Be careful of your head."

"I'm always careful," she giggles as she tumbles into the seat. "Oops. Except now."

She shuffles around a little bit and gets herself sat down normally and I shut the door and move around to the driver's side door. I get into the car and glance at Kerry.

"Put your seat belt on," I say.

"Why? Don't you trust your own driving?" she asks.

"Sure I do. It's everyone else around me that I don't trust," I smile.

She returns my smile and starts fumbling with the seat belt. After the fourth attempt, she finally manages to get a decent grip of it. She pulls it forward hard and it locks and she moans and slaps at it, chuntering away at it under her breath. I bite my lip to stop myself from laughing.

"Here, let me help you with that," I say.

"It's a little bit tricky isn't it?" she says.

"It sure is," I smile. Another lie, but a harmless lie designed to make Kerry feel better.

I lean over her and take the seat belt gently from her grip. I am conscious of the fact that I am leaning over her body, so close to her that I can smell the sweet smell of the gin on her breath. My hand brushes her breast as I pull the seat belt forward and I pull away quickly as though she has burned me. She laughs softly.

"You did that on purpose," she says.

"I swear I didn't," I tell her as I click the seat belt into place.

She flashes me a grin.

"I don't care if you did," she says. She reaches up with both hands and grabs a breast in each, pushing them together and lifting them slightly. "I have great boobs. Why wouldn't I want to share them with you."

I start the engine of the car, not sure what to even say to that. I force myself to look out of the wind shield and not at Kerry's amazing breasts.

"Blake?" Kerry says. I glance at her. She looks a little upset. She's released her breasts. "Don't you think I have nice boobs?"

"Of course I do," I tell her. "But if I'm looking at you instead of the road, we're likely to have an accident."

She seems to accept this and she nods her head and lets the subject of her breasts drop. I start to pull away when Kerry grabs my arm.

"Wait," she shouts, panic in her voice.

I slam the brakes on and look at her.

"What is it?" I ask.

She twists in her seat and looks into the back seat of the car and shakes her head.

"Where's Lisa? She's not in the car. Did we leave her behind somewhere?" she says looking at me in genuine horror.

"Lisa went home ages ago," I reassure her.

"Are you sure?" Kerry asks, eyeing me suspiciously like I might be lying to her.

"I'm certain," I say, nodding my head.

Kerry nods and then she starts unzipping her handbag and looking through it. She pulls her cell phone out as I start driving forwards again.

"I'm going to call her and see if she's really ok," she says.

"Well it's up to you, but I reckon she's probably in bed now and she won't be too happy if you wake her up for no good reason," I say.

Kerry considers this for a moment and then she nods and puts her cell phone back away.

"You're right. I'll call her in the morning," she says. "But when I do, if you're wrong and we did leave her behind, can we come back out here and get her?"

"Of course," I smile. "But I promise you I'm not wrong."

I'm not even going to consider trying to explain to her that if I was wrong and we left her behind here, she would just get a cab home. I hit the junction that adjoins the main road through the town and turn to Kerry.

"So where to?" I ask.

"Home James," she says, pointing out of the wind shield and laughing.

"Right," I laugh. "Which way is home?"

"To infinity and beyond," she says with a little nod of her head like this explains everything.

I roll my eyes and Kerry giggles.

"Left," she says. "I live to the left. 1218 Maple Street."

I turn left and Kerry falls silent looking out of the window. I glance back at her a few minutes later and see she has dozed off. I turn back to face the road, glad I have at least an idea where Maple Street is. I drive to Maple Street, pleased to learn that I was right in my assumption of where it is, and I slow down, watching the mail boxes, checking for number 1218. I spot it and pull up at the curb outside of the gate. I look over at Kerry. She's still asleep, her head back on the seat's headrest and her mouth hanging open.

I smile to myself and cut the engine. I get out of the car, slamming my door. That doesn't even wake Kerry up like I thought it would. I walk around the car to her side of it and open the passenger side door. I shake her shoulder gently.

"Kerry? You're home. Time to wake up," I say.

She doesn't respond and I shake her shoulder again. She makes a snorting sound and then turns her head slightly and starts snoring loudly. I don't think I have much chance of waking her up. I sigh and then I lean into the car and unclip her seat belt, being extra careful not to brush against her this time. It was bad enough doing that when she was awake. Doing it when she is asleep would make me feel like a total pervert.

I get the seat belt off her and scoop her up into my arms. I grab her hand bag off the floor and then I kick the car door shut. Kerry stirs long enough to wrap an arm around my neck and rest her head against my shoulder and then she falls asleep again, her breathing slow and deep.

I carry her down her garden path and pause at her front door. I don't like the idea of going through her handbag, but it's the only way I'm going to be able to find her front door key and so I awkwardly hold the handbag in my teeth and unzip it. I manage to find Kerry's keys and I zip her handbag up again. I try the first key and it doesn't fit the lock. The second key goes almost all of the way in and then it sticks. The third key I try goes into the lock smoothly and turns easily, unlocking the door.

I push the door open and take the key back out. I debate leaving Kerry in the lounge, but it's pretty chilly and I don't want her to get cold. I start up the stairs, carrying her with me. I reach the top and look into the first room I come to. It's a bathroom. The next one is a bedroom, but the bed isn't made up and I keep going. The next one looks like it's Kerry's room, and if it isn't, it'll have to do her for tonight.

I carry her into the room. There's a double bed in the middle of it, neatly made with white bedding. I lay Kerry down on the top of the bed and pull her shoes off. I draw the line at stripping her and I pull the duvet from the other side of the bed, covering Kerry with the part of it she isn't laying on. She stirs slightly, moaning in her sleep and then her eyes open and she smiles blearily at me.

"I think I'm a little bit drunk," she says, her voice still thick with sleep.

"Just a bit," I laugh. "Good night."

"Wait," she says. She reaches out and grabs my hand. "Stay with me until I fall back asleep."

I don't know quite what to say to that, but I figure it's not going to take long and so I sit down on the bed beside Kerry. She releases my hand and smiles up at me. Her eyes close but she opens them again and I reach down and stroke her cheek, brushing her hair back from it. She smiles again and then her eyes close and this time, she doesn't open them again. Within minutes, she's snoring again.

I know I should go, but I can't help but stay a moment longer, stroking Kerry's cheek and watching her sleep. She's so sweet when she's like this, drunk and happy. I wish she could be like this all of the time. But I know she won't be. Tomorrow she'll wake up full of regrets and her usual annoying self will re-emerge and ruin the conference for us both.

I sigh and stand up. I stop at the bedroom door and look back one more time. I stand for a moment watching Kerry sleep, memorizing how she looks when she's relaxed and peaceful, and then I slip down the stairs. I let myself out and check the door has locked behind me, and then I go to my car and get in.

I take a moment to just sit and think about tonight. Talk about a surreal night. I wasn't even going to bother going out. I only went out at all in the end because I was annoying myself berating myself for not going to Kerry's office to apologize to her sooner. By the time I had decided to stop letting my pride get in the way of doing the right thing and gone to her office, I was too late; she had already left for the day. I couldn't stop thinking about what an ass I had been and how it was going to make the weekend conference even more awkward than it was always going to be with Kerry and I going together. I went out to try and get a bit of light relief from the constant nagging thoughts about it in my head.

And who should I run into but Kerry. Kerry who I had never seen in that club before. Kerry who was somehow consuming all of my thoughts. And I hadn't been able to resist going to her after our eyes met and she stood looking at me, seemingly mesmerized by me, her chest heaving. And we'd had a fun night, a sexually charged fun night. And then this. I shake my head, hardly able to believe any of it has really happened.

I start the car engine and drive away from Kerry's place. I check the time as I head towards my apartment building. Seven minutes past three in the morning. I groan to myself. Getting up at six to catch our flight in the morning is looking less and less appealing by the minute. I can't help but laugh quietly to myself though. If it is going to be bad for me getting up so stupidly early after very little sleep, it is going to be even worse for Kerry with a hangover from hell on top of everything else.

I finally arrive home, glad I have already packed my suitcase for the next morning. I fall into bed without showering. I will shower in the morning. I don't expect to be able to sleep for thinking about Kerry, despite how tired I am, but I manage to fall asleep fairly quickly.

Kerry was sitting on the end of my bed, naked and glistening, her hair wet.

"Why are you wet?" I asked her.

"Because you turn me on so much," she replied.

I wanted to tell her that's not what I meant, but in that moment, it didn't matter. In that moment, all that mattered was Kerry naked and reaching out for me. I smiled as I went to her. She stood up and we wrapped our arms around each other, our lips meeting. She tasted of honey and sex, and as we kissed, she lifted herself, wrapping her legs around my waist.

I slipped into her, feeling her tightness around me. I started to thrust into her and I heard a shrill screaming sound. Was I hurting her?

My eyes fly open and I am no longer in Kerry's arms, no longer in her pussy. Instead, I am in my bed alone. The screeching sound is my alarm going off. I sigh in frustration, both at realizing that being with Kerry was only a dream and at being woken up while I am still so tired. I reach out and switch the alarm off, relieved when the shrill sound stops.

I yawn loudly, laying back against my pillow for a moment, not wanting to get up at all, but knowing that if I don't move pretty much straight away, I will likely fall back asleep and miss our flight. I don't want to try explaining to Mark that the one time I was to go to the conference instead of him, that I managed to sleep in and miss my flight. With that thought at the forefront of my mind, I push the duvet off me and get up before I can let my eyes close again.

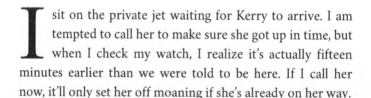

I sit on the private jet waiting for Kerry to arrive. I am tempted to call her to make sure she got up in time, but when I check my watch, I realize it's actually fifteen minutes earlier than we were told to be here. If I call her now, it'll only set her off moaning if she's already on her way.

I hear a noise behind me and glance over my shoulder. Kerry is making her way onto the plane, her overnight bag in her hand. She's wearing big sunglasses and I bite my lip trying not to smile at the thought of how hungover she must be to be wearing those to cover her eyes.

I look her up and down as she makes her way towards me, dragging the bag as it bounces off each seat she passes. She's wearing tight dark blue jeans, a black and white stripy top and a black suit jacket with three quarter sleeves. She looks good, there's no denying that.

"Good morning," I smile.

"Is it?" Kerry groans.

I stand up and try to take the bag from her but she snatches it away from me.

"I'm perfectly capable of putting my own luggage away thank you," she snaps.

I raise my hands in mock surrender and sit back down. I watch as Kerry fights the bag into the overhead storage compartment. Her top rides up ever so slightly showing me a flash of skin on her belly. It looks so soft and I feel myself wanting to reach out and touch it. I resist the urge and Kerry finally gets the bag stashed. She sits down opposite me.

"So how rough are you this morning then?" I ask with a grin.

Kerry doesn't answer for a second and I think she's going to ignore me but then she sighs and shrugs her shoulders.

"Have you ever seen a road in the middle of getting resur-faced, before they put the tar on the top?" she says. I nod. "I feel rougher than that surface."

I can't help but laugh. Kerry doesn't join in.

"I'm glad you think it's funny," she says.

"I kind of do," I say. "Call my laughter pay back for you throwing up over my shoes last night."

"Oh God, I didn't," Kerry says, looking at me in horror.

I laugh and shake my head.

"No, you didn't. But you were pretty far gone," I say.

"Bastard," she mumbles under her breath and then she smiles. "Yeah I was only meant to be going out for a couple, but the cocktails were flowing and one drink led to another, and well, now I have only myself to blame don't I."

"And maybe Lisa a little bit," I smile.

Kerry laughs softly.

"I like that plan. Yeah, it's all Lisa's fault," she says with a smile.

Her expression starts to harden suddenly, her smile gone.

"Anyway, thank you for the ride last night. I can assure you that you won't see me in that state ever again," she says.

I shrug.

"It's fine. We've all been there," I say.

Kerry grunts and turns away from me and I realize that our moment of chat is over. She has gone back to being the ice queen and to be honest, the reminder of what she's like when she's not drunk is enough to make me remember why I dislike her so much. She's haughty and I have never met anyone who moans as much as she does.

Yes, I can see now that even considering sleeping with her would be a mistake. Hell kissing her would be a mistake. It doesn't matter how soft and sensuous her lips look. It doesn't matter how good her body looks in those jeans. And it doesn't matter how pretty she is, she's bad news. I could never want to be with someone who gets on my last nerve as much as Kerry does. I mean if we were to ever do anything, I would have to keep her drunk all of the time just to tolerate her and that's not the basis for anything good.

"What?" Kerry demands, and I realize I have been staring at her. I look away quickly and shake my head. "Why are you staring at me?"

"It must be your magnetic charm drawing me in," I reply with a sarcastic smile.

"Ha, ha," Kerry says. "You're fucking hilarious."

The air stewardess approaches us then. She beams at me.

"Good morning Mr. Colton. Miss Morgan. How are you both?" she says.

"I'm great thanks Amber. How are you?" I ask.

"Oh good," she smiles. She smiles at Kerry who nods briefly at her but doesn't return her smile. "The captain will be taking off in the next few minutes so I just need you two to fasten your seat belts."

We both fasten our seat belts under Amber's watchful eye. She smiles approvingly and quickly runs through her safety spiel. When she's done, she goes and pulls the cabin door closed. The engines rumble into life and the captain's voice comes over the sound system. He tells us the flight duration and that we're in for a slightly bumpy ride due to a bit of high pressure. Kerry groans at the sound of that and I have to bite my lip to keep from grinning. She's really going to be miserable on this flight.

The sound system clicks off and the plane begins to move. After a few minutes, we start to rise. Kerry looks pretty white and she grips the arms rests tightly.

"Are you alright?" I ask her.

"Fine," she says through gritted teeth. "I just feel a bit sick. I'll be fine once we're up."

"That'll teach you not to down gin and tonics like they're soda," I laugh.

Kerry groans again and shakes her head.

"Don't even say the word gin," she says.

I want to wind her up a little bit more, but I really don't want her to throw up here so I stop talking and look out of the window. We soon level off and Kerry visibly relaxes. She reaches out and presses the button to call Amber who arrives quickly.

"Yes Miss Morgan?" she says.

"Can I get a coffee please Amber? Strong. Black. Two sugars," Kerry says.

Amber's smile slips ever so slightly as she responds.

"I'm afraid we don't have any refreshments on board Miss Morgan," she says.

"What? Why not?" Kerry demands.

"Well it's company policy. It's only a twenty minute flight and we would end up wasting too much stuff," Amber replies.

"That's crazy," Kerry snaps.

"Let it go," I say, cutting Kerry off before she can say anything else. "It's no good being a bitch to Amber. It's not her policy."

"I'm not being a bitch, I'm just saying that…" Kerry says.

"That you can't wait fifteen minutes for a coffee. Yeah I heard," I interrupt her again. I turn to Amber and flash her a smile. "Thanks Amber, we're all good."

Amber scurries away looking relieved as Kerry glares at me.

"What the fuck is your problem?" she snaps at me.

"I'll let you take a guess," I reply.

I can't see Kerry's eyes for the sunglasses, but I'd bet my last dollar that she's rolling them. She turns her head away from me and reclines her seat. I turn to look out the window. I am more than happy to ignore her. I can't believe that for a few hours last night, I actually thought that it was possible that beneath the ice queen exterior, there was a nice person in there. That's like saying that underneath it all, Hitler wasn't such a bad guy. Ok, maybe it's going a little bit too far to compare Kerry to Hitler, but honestly, I'll be glad when it's Sunday evening and we're back home from the conference.

The rest of the flight passes in silence until the captain's voice comes over the loudspeaker again, announcing that we're about to land. I keep looking out of the window, determined to ignore Kerry and not let her ruin the conference for me. This is the first one I've been to and I really don't want it to be ruined by the company I am being forced to keep.

We land and get off the plane. I have learned from experience not to offer to help Kerry with her bag, not that I want to now anyway. We climb down the stairs of the plane and cross the tarmac to our waiting car, neither of us speaking a word to each other. The driver gets out of the car and opens the trunk for our luggage.

"Good morning sir, ma'am," he says.

Kerry and I both greet him and then we get into the car. The driver gets back in and takes us to the hotel. Again, Kerry and I refrain from speaking to each other, each of us sitting looking out of the window on our side of the car. I can't help but wonder what the driver makes of us sitting there in stony silence this way. Maybe he's just relieved that he doesn't have to sit through any inane chatter.

We arrive at the hotel and retrieve our luggage. We both thank the driver who nods to us and then drives away, leaving us outside of the hotel. The hotel is the Hotel Delaney, the place where the conference is to be held. I check the time. It's getting on for eight and the conference starts at ten. That will give us plenty of time to get checked in and unpack and everything.

We step inside of the hotel. It's cool in the lobby, the air conditioning blasting out. The hotel has that quiet feeling that nice hotels always seem to have, no matter how busy they are. The lobby is almost deserted this early though. One person stands waiting for the elevator and the receptionist and the porter are talking quietly over the desk and there is no sign of anyone else.

We head for the desk and the receptionist smiles a greeting at us.

"Good morning. Welcome to the Hotel Delaney. How can I help you?" she says.

"Hi. We have two rooms booked for Colton and Morgan Co," I tell her.

"One moment sir," she smiles.

She clacks on her keyboard for a moment and then she frowns. She clacks a couple more times and then she looks up at me.

"I'm afraid your reservation is only for one room sir," she says.

"No that can't be right," I say. "It's definitely for two rooms. Please check again."

She looks like she wants to argue with me, but she goes back to her computer and clacks on it again. She looks up and shakes her head.

"It's definitely only one room sir," she says. "I can see you did have two rooms booked, but one of them was cancelled early last week."

"Cancelled?" Kerry says, speaking for the first time since we came in here. "By whom?"

"I'm sorry, it doesn't say," the receptionist replies.

"So anyone can call at any time and just cancel someone else's booking?" Kerry demands. "Because neither of us made that call."

"If they have all of the details of the booking then they can cancel it, yes. We work on the assumption that our guests don't give out their booking details to people who might choose to cancel their reservation for no reason," the receptionist replies.

Her smile hasn't slipped, but her tone has become icy as she regards Kerry and her attitude. Kerry makes a snorting noise down her nose.

"Are you suggesting that we gave our details to someone irresponsibly?" she snaps.

"Not at all," the receptionist replies. "I'm merely informing you that to cancel the booking, the person needs all of the reservation information."

Kerry turns to me and glares at me.

"This is your fault," she says.

I am taken aback by the insinuation and I shake my head.

"How the hell do you work that out?" I demand. "Your assistant was the one who was tasked with booking the rooms. Who did she give the details to?"

"She understands discretion," Kerry says. She turns back to the receptionist. "We need to book a second room please."

"I'm sorry ma'am. With the conference, we're completely full tonight," the receptionist says.

KERRY

I blink hard and my mouth drops open when the receptionist informs me that the entire hotel is full tonight. This has to be some sort of a mistake. It has to be. Oh God, please let it be a mistake.

"You have to be joking," I say. "You must have something available."

"I'm sorry, we don't have any rooms at all vacant tonight," the receptionist repeats.

Her customer service smile stays in place, but I'd be willing to bet she's ready to throttle me. It's really irritating when people insist you're wrong without any idea of what they're talking about, but I just couldn't help it this time. It wasn't that I thought she was lying to me; I was just so desperate for her to be wrong.

"I can call around some of the other local hotels and see if they have anything, but I have to say I would be surprised if they do. This is one of the busiest weekends of the year for all of the hotels in this area," the receptionist adds.

"That would be great, thank you" I say, smiling at her, crossing my fingers that she manages to find us something.

The receptionist gives me a frosty smile and a curt nod of her head. I think she wanted me to tell her that calling around all of the other local hotels didn't matter but I can't do that because it does matter. At least to me it does. It matters very much. I can't possibly share a room with Blake. I don't know what would happen first – us killing each other or us fucking each other – and neither of them are something that I particularly want to have happen this weekend or ever for that matter.

I turn to Blake and roll my eyes as the receptionist starts making the promised calls.

"I can't believe this has happened," I say. "I can't see who would have tried to cancel our booking. I think it's a glitch in their system and they just won't admit to making a mistake personally."

"I think you're clutching at straws a little bit there Kerry," Blake says.

"Why?" I demand. "I mean surely if someone from the firm tried to cancel the booking, the hotel should have called one of us to confirm that was correct."

"Sure," Blake says with that infuriating smile. "Because we have nothing better to do than to go back over jobs we've asked our assistants to take care of. We'd be so annoyed if everyone wanted our confirmation of every little thing."

"Right, fine," I say. "But at the very least they should confirm things with us when it's obvious they weren't something we would have ordered."

Blake laughs and starts to open his mouth and I shake my head and raise my hand.

"Don't," I say. "I heard it."

As if the hotel staff would know what orders were genuine. How would they know what we did or didn't want? If they did, we wouldn't need assistants at all.

"I just can't believe this has happened," I say shaking my head. "This is the most important weekend of the year for realtors and somehow someone has managed to have a screw up occur before we even get started."

"You mean you managed to have a screw up before we even get started," Blake says, still smiling that infuriating smile of his, the one that makes me simultaneously want to punch him and throw myself against his body and kiss him.

"No I didn't screw this up," I snap. "Don't you think it's strange that I have been coming here for years with my father and nothing has ever gone wrong? Not with the book-ings or the check in, or anything at all. Yet the one time you're involved, this happens."

"I fail to see how you can associate this mistake with me considering I had nothing at all to do with the booking of the rooms," Blake says.

He's right, but just the fact he had to point it out makes me angry and I refuse to acknowledge that he's right. Instead, I make a frustrated groaning sound and look away from him. I really could punch him right now, right in that smug little mouth of his. And then maybe I could kiss him, make the pain go away. I shake away the thought. The last thing I need is thoughts like that about Blake right now. I need to stick firmly to the wanting to punch him part of the thought.

Instead of thinking about Blake and how he irritates me and turns me on in almost equal measures, I try to focus on the receptionist and her conversations with the other local hotels. It's clear from her expression that she's having no luck with any of them. I sigh. Dammit. It's all going to end in disaster, that much is becoming clearer to me by the minute.

The only good thing to come from all of this is that the stress of it all seems to have shifted my hangover so at least I might be able to enjoy the conference. Once I get past the sheer horror of the idea of having to share a room with Blake.

"I'm sorry," the receptionist says, putting the receiver of her phone down and not picking it back up again this time. "I've tried every hotel in the region and they're all fully booked. I can try further out for you but you're looking at a two or three hour drive to get to them even if they can fit you in."

I shake my head.

"That's no good," I say. "We don't have a car here."

"Ok," the receptionist says.

She doesn't say anything else. She just stands there looking at me with a questioning smile and I realize she has genuinely done everything she can do and now she's waiting to see if we're going to take the room or yell at her and leave. I feel like yelling at Blake and leaving to be honest, but that's not going to solve anything. I look at Blake.

"I guess we'll have to share the room," I say.

"Yeah, you can take the floor," he winks.

I roll my eyes and turn back to the receptionist who tries and fails to hide her amusement at Blake's comment. I ignore her almost grin.

"I guess we'll just have to make the best of it. We'll check in now please. Can we get two keys for the room please?" I say.

"Of course ma'am," the receptionist replies. "No problem at all. Just give me one second."

She goes back to her computer and types a few things in and then she turns behind her and grabs two keycards from a hook on a board there. She holds them out to us and Blake and I take one each.

"You're in room 203. You'll find it on the second floor on the right hand side of the corridor. The elevators are just there behind you and the stairs are through the door beside them. The restaurant where all of the hotel's meals are served is down there and then to the left," she says, pointing down a corridor beside the reception desk. "The bar is down there and to the right. And perhaps most importantly for you, the conference is taking place on the top floor."

She pauses and takes a breath and I realize she's said all of her spiel so far on one long breath. I am more than a little bit impressed at her lung capacity if I'm being honest.

"If you need anything, don't hesitate to call down to reception. Just hit zero on your room's phone," the receptionist adds, still with her smile in place. "I hope you both enjoy your stay."

"Fat chance of that," I mumble under my breath.

I force myself to smile at the receptionist. In fairness, none of this is her fault and she's handled me being pissed off about it all way better than I would have in her place.

"Thank you," I manage to say grudgingly, reminding myself once more that even if the hotel screwed up our booking, that's not her fault.

She smiles back at me, a genuine smile that holds more than a little bit of relief. I'm not sure if it's because she now thinks I'm less likely to complain to her manager about this now that I'm acting a bit less cold, or if it's because I'm finally moving away from her desk. It's probably the latter and I don't really blame her. I mean two adults having to share a room for one night is hardly a big deal and it's not like she knows the situation with Blake and why the idea of sharing a room with him had me acting out so much.

"You're welcome," the receptionist says to me, still smiling.

I don't really think I am welcome at all, but I only have myself to blame for that and so I flash her another smile, one I hope is at least a little bit apologetic looking, and then I turn away from the reception desk and cross the lobby and head for the elevators. Blake hurries to catch up with me as one of the elevator's doors open and I step inside and hit the number two button. He gets in and shakes his head as the doors close behind him.

"What?" I say.

"Nothing," he mutters, rolling his eyes and looking down at his shoes.

"Come on, spit it out," I say. "You're standing there shaking your head and rolling your eyes. At least be grown up enough to tell me what I'm meant to have done."

"It's just the way you're going on," he says. "You're acting like you're the only one who is put out by this. Just so you know, I'm not exactly thrilled about the idea of us only having one room for tonight myself."

It kind of stings to hear that Blake isn't happy about the idea of sharing a room with me and I ask myself why. I mean I don't want to share a room with him either and I know I'm hardly his favorite person in the world. So why would he be happy about it? I knew he wouldn't be happy about it and logically I get why, but hearing him say it out loud still hurts a bit. I shrug my shoulders, covering my hurt with what I hope is a slightly annoyed looking expression.

"You didn't seem to mind the idea too much downstairs or you would have opened your mouth and helped me out a bit," I say.

Blake rolls his eyes again and this time, he at least looks at me as he speaks.

"I could have stood and yelled at the receptionist all day and then demanded to see a manager and yelled at him or her too, but what use would it have been Kerry? Huh? None that's how much. It's not like it would have changed the fact that they don't have another room," he points out.

"Whatever," I sigh, hating to admit that he's right and I'm just being petulant because he admitted to not wanting to share the room with me.

I'm glad when the elevator reaches our floor and the doors ping open and I step out into the corridor. I glance at the sign and follow the arrow pointing towards the rooms in the low two hundreds. I find the right door on the right hand side of the corridor where the receptionist told me it would be, and I push my key card into the slot in the handle and then I open the room up.

I step inside and look around. The room is clean and fairly big. It has a big double bed with crisp, clean looking white sheets and pillow cases, a wardrobe, a chest of drawers, a desk and a small armchair. It would be more than adequate to share with someone I actually want to share a room with. In fact, I would go as far as to say it would be pretty much ideal to share with someone I wanted to share a room with. There's nothing at all wrong with the room; only the company I need to keep whilst I'm in it.

I move away from the door, into the center of the room and I put my bag down on the bed for a moment and then I go and peer into the en suite bathroom. It's smallish but it's equipped well with a toilet, a sink and a bath and a shower. It has a small basket of toiletries on the shelf that sits around the sink and it also has several white fluffy towels hanging on the towel rail beside the bath. The room looks like it is spotlessly clean and again it would be perfectly good to share with someone other than Blake. I sigh as I move back into the main room and begin to open up my bag.

"Well I guess we'd better get unpacked and freshen up for the conference," I say, more to break the silence that's fallen between Blake and I than anything else.

I don't want to be here like this any more than he does, but we're stuck with the arrangement now and we might as well make the best of it instead of being awkward and nasty to each other the whole time. He nods his head thoughtfully and then he glances at his watch and checks the time.

"Yeah we really should. We've wasted most of the time we had to get sorted for the conference downstairs arguing with the receptionist so we'd best hurry up," he says.

He's agreeing with me and yet I still feel as though he's somehow having a go at me, like it's my fault we got held up or something. I mean yes, I was the one who did the talking, and I know Blake would have had the receptionist call around and ask about another room too. It still would have taken the same amount of time if he took the lead in the check in conversation.

I debate telling him that, but I decide against it and in the end, I don't comment on what he's said at all. Instead, I just give him a nod of my head to let him know I agree that we need to hurry up a bit. If I try to explain to him that he would have taken the same amount of time as I did getting us checked in, he'll just agree with me and then when I tell him he sounded like he was accusing me of wasting our time and holding us up, he'll only deny it and then I'll look like I'm being paranoid.

Maybe I am being paranoid. I don't know. It's certainly possible. Maybe I'm being overly sensitive because of Blake's comments about not wanting to share the room with me. Or maybe it's simpler than that. Maybe it's just a case of my hangover not being quite gone after all and the leftover stale alcohol in my system is leaving me feeling a little bit emotionally sensitive. Yeah, that's most likely it.

That has to be it surely. I mean I know I don't usually get emotional or particularly sensitive when I have a hangover, but it's still a much more likely explanation for the way I'm feeling right now than it being because I suddenly care about what Blake thinks of me and his opinion on our sleeping arrangements. And it's certainly an easier pill to swallow than the one where I have started to care whether or not Blake wants to spend time with me would be. I don't even want to think about that as a possibility for why I'm letting this bother me so much, let alone admit to myself that's exactly what it is.

I push the thoughts away and concentrate on getting sorted for the conference. I start to pull my things out of my bag as Blake lifts his bag up onto the bed beside mine. I grab my toiletries' bag and my make-up bag and I take them into the bathroom. As I come back out of the bathroom and step out into the main part of the room, Blake is on his way into the bathroom, and for a second, we are pressed up against each other as we pass in the doorway. I feel my chest brushing against his, and I feel my breath catch in my throat as my body responds to his closeness, my pussy instantly wet as my nipples tingle from the touch of his muscular chest against them.

I look down at the ground as I move away from Blake, feeling heat rising to my cheeks.

"Sorry," I mutter.

I don't think he's heard me until I hear him reply, telling me it's fine. It sure felt like it was more than fine. It felt amazing for a moment there.

God what the hell is wrong with me? I can't even blame the booze for this one. There's no getting around it. No matter how much Blake might annoy me, I am completely and utterly in lust with him. I am getting more attracted every time I see him and my body is determined to betray me and continue to want Blake even as my head tries to persuade me that's not a good idea.

I turn all of my attention back to my bag to avoid having to look at Blake as he comes back into the main room. I start pulling my clothes out of the bag and I go to the wardrobe and pull it open. I feel a bit more in control now and I reach up to hang my things up and then I sigh. There are no hangers. Just great.

"For fuck sake," I curse, annoyed at the lack of hangers and also annoyed that I debated bringing some and then talked myself out of it, telling myself the hotel was bound to have some in the wardrobe for me to use.

"What is it?" Blake asks.

"There are no hangers," I say, glancing back over my shoulder at him.

He shrugs his shoulders like it's not a big deal.

"It's not the end of the world Kerry," he says.

"I didn't say it was, but where am I meant to hang my dress?

"Just lay it over the bed or the chair," he says.

I'm not happy at the idea, but I don't have much other choice unless I want to go down to reception and ask for hangers. I will then have to wait for them to arrive and I'll likely miss the start of the conference. That will just give Blake a reason to have a go at me.

I sigh and lay the dress as carefully as I can across the bed. I put the rest of my stuff in a drawer in the dresser– my underwear and my clothes for the flight home tomorrow, stuff I'm not that worried about the possibility of creasing – and I leave the other three drawers empty for Blake to use.

Blake is whistling to himself as he puts his things into the drawers I've left him. I don't know what he's suddenly so happy about. This is hardly the arrangement either of us would have chosen and he's made it quite clear he agrees with me on that score. I guess he's just making the best of a bad situation. I suppose really I should try to do the same. I mean what's the worst thing that can happen? I don't allow myself to answer that question.

I go over to the closed floor length curtains and pull them open, ready to pop out onto the balcony for a quick breath of fresh air before I go back into the bathroom and freshen up. I am stopped in my tracks when the curtains part and I see not a door, but a window.

"We don't have a balcony," I say, glancing over my shoulder at Blake.

"Huh?" he says, looking up from one of the drawers.

"We don't have a balcony in our room. It's just a window," I repeat, nodding to the window in front of me.

"Ah well. We're only here for one night," he shrugs.

"I know, but I specifically asked for a room with a balcony. We'll have to remember to check the bill and just make sure that we're not charged for a balcony," I say.

Blake nods his head.

"Yeah, we will," he says. He nods towards the bathroom. "Do you want to be in there or should I go first?"

"You go," I say.

I turn back to look out of the window as Blake goes into the bathroom. It's not a bad view and at least the sun is shining. I really would like to be able to go out onto my balcony and enjoy the bit of sun though. I go and lay down on the bed for a moment. It's nice and soft and comfortable and I think I could have a good night's sleep here if I was alone.

I must have managed to fall asleep anyway because I wake up as the bathroom door closes. I sit up and rub my face.

"I hope you haven't been drooling on my bed there," Blake says.

I glance at him. His eyes are twinkling with humor and he looks hot with his hair freshly styled. I feel myself wanting to go to him so badly, but I resist the urge. I smile back at Blake.

"I figured if I did you'd have to let me take the bed," I say.

"And deprive you of the floor? No, I wouldn't dream of it," Blake says.

"So chivalrous," I laugh as I get up off the bed and head for the bathroom. "I won't be long."

I lock the bathroom door behind me. I use the toilet and then I clean my teeth. The water is freezing cold and I'm glad I have already showered at home this morning. I quickly touch up my makeup and comb my hair through and then I go back into the room.

"The water is freezing," I say. "Did you notice?"

"It was fine for me. Maybe I used up all of the hot water we had, sorry," Blake says.

I shrug my shoulders.

"It's fine. I only really brushed my teeth. I just hope it's hot in the morning," I say. "The last thing I'm going to want is to get up to a cold shower. Mind you, they managed to mess up our reservation and the room type. Not to mention the lack of hangers. It really wouldn't surprise me too much if the water never gets hot. I guess I should just prepare myself for it."

"For the love God can you shut up?" Blake shouts.

I stare at him in surprise. I knew I was babbling a bit, but I really don't think there was any need for that. I am too shocked at him yelling at me to even answer him. I just stand there looking at him, my mouth hanging open in shock.

"Honestly Kerry, all you've done all morning is complain and I'm sick to death of it," Blake says.

He's not yelling now. Instead, he's speaking to me in a quiet voice, but rather than it being a quiet voice that says he's ashamed of himself, it's the sort of quiet voice that says he's speaking to someone so unreasonable that it's a waste of time even bothering to get angry at them. I hate that he feels that way about me, yet I still can't stop myself from snapping back at him. I mean I might have been a bit moany, but I feel like it was justified. Everything I've moaned about has actually happened; it's not like I'm just moaning for the sake of it.

"Well excuse me for caring that our booking is wrong," I snap. "This isn't a cheap hotel Blake and I expect better from them, that's all I'm saying."

"You still don't get it do you? Our booking? It's not wrong. I didn't ask for a balcony. Obviously the balcony room is the one that got cancelled. Now listen here. I've tried to treat you as an equal but I'm afraid I'm going to have to put my foot down. You're not on vacation here Kerry. You're here for work. You're being paid to be here and represent the company, and I don't want anyone leaving this conference thinking that we're all moaning snobs. Am I making myself clear?" Blake says.

"Perfectly," I say coolly.

I turn away from Blake and pick up my handbag and my room key and I head out of the room. I have nothing more to say to Blake after his little tantrum back there. He can go and rot in hell as far as I'm concerned. I tell myself the thickening in my throat is because I'm angry at being spoken to like a child, not because I'm upset that Blake seems to hate me even more than usual.

I hear the room door open and close behind me.

"Kerry. Kerry, wait," Blake shouts along the corridor after me.

I keep walking, not looking back. I'm past even caring if I'm being childish or not. I can't deal with Blake right now. I'm done with him. Done.

"Look I'm sorry. I went too far," he adds from behind me.

I still don't look back. I walk straight past the elevators and head to the stairs and I make my way up to the fifth floor. I quickly move into the room where the opening speeches will be held and I find a seat that has people on either side of it so that Blake can't try to get himself sat down next to me and force me to hear him out. I fix my gaze on the back of the chair in front of me, not looking up in case I accidently catch Blake's eyes. He's reminded me of why I hate him so much and I want nothing more to do with him this weekend or ever.

~

I have done a good job of avoiding Blake all day. I have to wonder if he was purposely avoiding me too. We have both spent the day attending the various talks and demonstrations and socializing with other people in the business. For us not to have ran into each other at some point, it definitely makes me think that it wasn't accidental and that Blake has been trying to avoid me every bit as much as I have been trying to avoid him.

I don't know how to feel about that. I know I should be happy about it; it's not like I want to see Blake at all. But despite that, there's a small part of me that's a little bit upset that Blake is avoiding me instead of trying to apologize for what he said to me this morning. I mean I know he did try to apologize straight after saying it and I refused to hear him out, but I guess I figured he would try again later on in the day, and maybe once I had had a little bit of time to calm down a bit, that I might have actually heard him out that time.

Oh well. I'm not going to let it worry me. And I'm not going to let it ruin this evening for me either. The conference is always a good day, but it's always a better evening. Everyone lets their hair down a little bit and has fun and it's a great excuse to catch up with everyone in the business, meet some new people, and yes, get a bit tipsy.

I have been up to our room and showered and changed, and still I didn't run into Blake. I'm kind of glad, because my dress isn't creased at all and he would have been presented with a perfect 'I told you so' moment after I protested about the wardrobe not having any hangers.

I shake off the thought of Blake and him being right – I won't let him ruin this evening for me – and I get into the elevator now and make my way down to the bar where the fun will be starting any time now. I am wearing a cornflower blue dress, a dress short enough to show my legs off but not short enough to look out of place at a professional event, and high black heels. I tell myself I don't care if Blake sees me dressed up or not, but it's a lie. I do care. I want him to see me. I want him to want me. Not that I will act on it even if he does. Or will I? I don't even know anymore. God I hate Blake. I hate how he's in my head even when he's not in my line of sight.

I sigh and shake my head, pushing all thoughts of Blake away. The elevator reaches the ground floor and I step out and head for the bar. It's still pretty quiet and a quick glance around reveals that none of the guys I know from the past years' conferences are here yet. I sit down at the bar and order a glass of white wine which I sit and sip while I wait for some others who I know to start to arrive. I'm sure it won't be long. I am a little bit early, but I know I won't be the only one who arrives early.

"Good evening," a voice says from beside me and I glance up from my glass.

A man is sitting on the bar stool beside mine. Even seated I can see that he would be tall. He's cute - blonde haired and good looking with a sharp jawline and cute little dimples. His eyes sparkle as he looks at me.

"Good evening," I reply with a smile.

"Are you here for the conference?" the man asks me, signaling to the bartender at the same time.

I nod and extend my hand.

"Kerry Morgan. Colton and Morgan Co," I tell him.

"Ooh, the owner of the company," he grins, shaking my hand. He turns to the bartender. "A vodka and tonic and another one for the lady please."

I have barely made a dent on the drink I already have in front of me, but I don't object. Instead, I smile my thanks at the man.

"I'm Rob Carlisle. I work for Jackson and Hart," he smiles.

"I've heard of them," I say. "And just so you know, I'm not the owner of Colton and Morgan Co. That would be my father."

"Ah you're one of the lucky ones. Getting a job easily because your dad is an owner," Rob says.

He doesn't say it in a nasty way, he says it in a teasing way, his eyes sparkling again and his mouth curling up in a cheeky smile. I smile back at him.

"Or you could say my dad is one of the lucky ones. Having a daughter who is also a damned good realtor when he just so happens to have a real estate firm," I say.

"I like that way of looking at it," Rob says, nodding his approval.

"Me too," I agree. "Now I just have to get my dad's partner to see it that way and we're all good."

I sense someone behind me and I turn around to see who it is. My heart flutters strangely when I see Blake sliding onto the bar stool on the other side of me. I'm not sure if I feel the strange flutters in my chest and my stomach because I'm excited to see him or if it's because I'm pissed off that he's here. He flashes me a smile.

"I thought I'd find you here," he says.

"You make me sound like some sort of an alcoholic," I say with a smile.

I'm far from ready to forgive and forget after the way Blake went on this morning, but I don't want to act like a bitch in front of Rob.

"Those are your words not mine," Blake grins.

The bartender approaches Blake and grateful for the interruption, I turn back to Rob.

"How long have you been in the business Rob?" I ask.

"About seven years," Rob says.

"That long?" I say, raising an eyebrow. "I'm shocked I don't recognize you from any of the other conferences."

"It's my first time at the conference actually. My boss couldn't make it and I got roped in at the last minute," Rob says.

"Ah well that explains it then," I smile. "Because I'm sure I would have remembered you."

Rob smiles back at me and for a moment, something passes between us. An unspoken agreement that there might be something here.

"Aren't you going to introduce us?" Blake says from beside me, ruining the moment between Rob and I.

I sigh and grit my teeth, warning myself to be polite and not to let Rob see the tension between Blake and I. I want to just say no and carry on talking to Rob, but that would make me look rude and I don't want Rob to think I'm someone to avoid.

"Blake Colton, this is Rob Carlisle," I say. "He works for Jackson and Hart."

Blake leans across me and he and Rob shake hands.

"Nice firm," Blake says.

"Yeah. I like it," Rob says. "So I take it you're the co-owner at Kerry's firm then?"

Blake nods his head.

"Yup. I'm her boss so she had better be on her best behaviour tonight," he says.

I roll my eyes and then I glare at Blake, trying to make him see that this is inappropriate. He picks his drink up and takes a sip and I think he's taken the hint. I turn back to Rob, putting my back to Blake, making sure there's no way he can misunderstand the message I'm sending him.

"I'm not so sure I'm going to be on my best behaviour," I say. "It's not like we're actually at work is it?"

Rob grins at me and shakes his head and I feel guilty for a moment, like I am using him to make Blake jealous. Maybe I am. Or maybe I really do just want Blake to go away and leave me alone. I barely know myself what I want anymore.

But I know that for whatever reason, I said that loud enough for Blake to hear me.

The thing is with Blake, just when I start to think that maybe I misjudged him and he isn't so bad after all, he says or does something that reminds me why I disliked him so much in the first place. And that throws me, leaving my head reeling, but not as much as it reels when he does something nice and leaves me unsure of whether or not I am actually justified in hating him. God why does this have to be so complicated. I've never met anyone who can make me feel such conflicting things for them, sometimes at the same time as each other too.

I am letting Blake get into my head again, even now while I'm sitting here with a cute guy who is obviously interested in me and isn't being a dick about it. I have to let this ridiculous obsession with Blake go. It barely even matters if I decide I like him or I hate him. Nothing will happen between us either way. I force him out of my head and focus on Rob, realizing he's been talking to me and I have no idea what he has said.

I smile and nod, trying to bluff my way through the conversation. Rob laughs and I frown slightly, kicking myself on the inside. What the hell have I just agreed to?

"You have no idea what I just said do you?" Rob asks.

Sheepishly, I shake my head.

"No. Sorry. I kind of spaced out there," I admit.

"I figured," Rob said. "So I asked you if you had ever been to another planet. You nodded your head. So tell me about your trip to outer space."

He's grinning and I realize he's not pissed off that I spaced out for a moment and missed what he was saying. I decide to play along.

"Well," I start. "It was a couple of months ago. I…"

"She's always spaced out," Blake interrupts, leaning across me to look at Rob with a conspiratorial grin that I don't like one little bit. "You get used to it though."

I glare at Blake, annoyed that he has cut me off mid sentence, but even more annoyed that he's purposely said something that makes it sound like we know each other really well. Rob smiles, looking a little bit uncomfortable. If Blake notices Rob's discomfort, which I'm sure he does, he ignores it and goes right on.

"Yeah. She's a dreamer, our Kerry," Blake laughs. "Always has her head in the clouds."

"That's so not true," I say, regaining my composure. "I'm really not one of those dreamy people that go off into a world of their own. I prefer to see what's actually out there, even if it's something I would rather not see."

I glare pointedly at Blake on the last part, but he makes no effort to move. Rob clears his throat and takes a long drink of his drink, clearly still uncomfortable. Fuck.

"Seriously," I add, focusing on Rob. "Just ignore Blake. It looks like he's had a drink or two too many and he starts to think he's funny when he's not."

Blake snorts out a laugh from behind me. A laugh I ignore.

"So Rob, where did you grow up?" I ask, moving the conversation on from Blake as quickly as I can without really stopping to think about what I'm actually saying.

I could kick myself once the words are out of my mouth. I know immediately that it's a lame question. So lame. But I couldn't think of anything else to say in the moment and I wanted to move the conversation on from Blake's interruption so badly that I just panicked and blurted out the first thing that came into my head. I couldn't just sit silent though, because I know that if Blake thinks he's annoying me, he'll stick around and interrupt all the more. If he thinks he's having no effect on me, he'll get bored and go away eventually. Sooner rather than later I hope.

"California," Rob replies. "At least I was born there and we lived there until I was seven. After that, we moved to Phoenix and I've lived there ever since."

"That's quite a difference," I smile.

"Yeah. Even now I sometimes crave the laid back Californian attitude. I go back a couple of times a year to visit some family and stuff though, and that's usually enough for me. What about you? Where did you grow up?" Rob says.

"New York," I say. "Born and bred."

"And you've lived there all of your life?" Rob says, looking surprised.

"Sure," I say. "When you live in the best city in the world, why would you want to move?"

"I take it from that then you enjoy living in New York?" Rob smiles.

"Oh I love it," I gush. "I love that there's always something going on. I love that even in the dead of night, there are people about and they're not necessarily crazies. I love the hustle and bustle, the tourists and the crowds."

"You love what pretty much everyone I know from New York says they hate," Rob laughs.

I laugh with him and shrug my shoulders.

"Yeah. I guess I'm a bit weird that way. But yeah, New York is kind of an acquired taste," I say.

"That's why us New Yorkers tend to stick together. We understand each other in a way outsiders just don't get," Blake interrupts us.

"Ah well, maybe I would get it," Rob smiles. "Maybe I would visit New York and instantly fall in love with it."

"Maybe. But it's still different being a local to a long term tourist," Blake says.

Rob laughs and shakes his head.

"Such a snob," he says. "Looking down on the tourists. I bet you're one of those people who go on a vacation and insist they are a traveler not a tourist."

Rob puts the word traveler in air quotes and Blake blushes slightly. I bite my bottom lip to keep from grinning. I have heard Blake use the word traveling to describe his vacations myself and I have always laughed at how ridiculous it sounds. It's good to hear someone else calling him out on it.

"It's not that I look down on tourists," Blake says, recovering from his moment of being thrown. "I mean they have their place and that. But they'll never really get the city the way we do. It'll never be in their blood. And I guess that means they'll never really be able to handle a true New Yorker."

"You make it sound like you're all feral or something," Rob laughs. He turns his attention to me. "Are you feral Kerry? Do I need to tame you?"

"Oh absolutely," I grin. "But don't worry. I'm house trained. I just have a nasty habit of biting."

I wink and snap my teeth in Rob's direction. I am definitely flirting now and I still don't know for sure if I'm doing it because I want Rob or because I want to annoy Blake some more like he's annoying me. Maybe it's both. I mean Rob is definitely cute and normally, I would definitely be interested in him. But now I seem to be more interested in Blake, someone I would normally have gladly ignored. Ugh this is like torture.

I decide I'm being stupid. Blake and I might have a bit of chemistry, but that's it. We don't click as people whereas Rob and I do so far. I decide to block Blake out completely and concentrate on getting to know Rob. And if things go well, who knows. Maybe I'll be sharing a room with him tonight instead of sharing it with Blake.

Rob and I chat for a little bit longer and he orders us another round of drinks. Blake doesn't interrupt us and I am starting to think he's gotten bored of the game now that he's realized that he's not really bothering either me or Rob. My heart sinks when Blake taps me on the shoulder and I realize I was wrong. I turn to glance at him, the smile slipping from my face.

"What?" I demand.

"Is that anyway to speak to a friend?" Blake smiles.

"No. But you're not a friend. I'm kind of busy here Blake. What do you want?" I say.

"I was just thinking maybe we should get an early night ready for our flight tomorrow. I would hate for you to end up in a state like you did the other night. Remember how rough you felt on the way out here?" Blake says.

He's smiling, the picture of innocence, but I know what he's doing and I know that he knows it too. He's making it sound like I'm some sort of crazy drunk, and the idea of us both having an early night implies there's some intimacy between us, that maybe we'd be having an early night together.

I force myself to smile back at Blake, aware that if I over react, I will only make myself look crazy.

"I'm ok, but thanks for your concern. You feel free to go on up and get an early night though. I'm sure I'll be just fine with Rob," I say.

"She will," Rob confirms.

"But…" Blake starts.

"You know, you're pretty concerned about what Kerry does and doesn't do. Are you sure you're not more than just her boss?" Rob says.

"I'm just looking out for her," Blake says. He looks away from us and orders another drink. Great. So much for him disappearing and leaving me alone. "Her dad wouldn't be happy if I let anything bad happen to her."

"Well you can relax. I have no intention of doing anything bad to her," Rob says. He lowers his voice and leans in close to me. "At least not unless you ask me nicely."

I laugh and put my hand on his knee.

"Maybe I will," I say.

Rob is still leaning in close to me and talking in a low voice.

"He's into you you know," he says, nodding towards Blake.

"Oh trust me he isn't," I say. "He just likes to try and make my life hell."

"Trust me, that's not what this is. He's jealous," Rob says.

I feel myself flushing slightly. Is Blake really jealous? Is he trying to get Rob to disappear, not to piss me off, but to keep me for himself? No. It's too crazy. He's just being his usual asshole self. I refuse to believe it can be anything more than that, because I refuse to let myself hope for anything more than that. My pussy has other ideas. It floods at the idea of Blake being jealous of Rob.

"Well he'll just have to get over it won't he," I say to Rob, ignoring the tingling in my clit.

We go back to chatting and while I am conscious of Blake still sitting there, his eyes on me, he doesn't say anything else and I force myself to focus only on Rob. It's not easy, but I manage it, telling myself I'm not doing it to get a reaction out of Blake. I'm not doing it to see if Blake really is jealous. I'm doing it because I like Rob and I want to spend the night with him. I wonder how many times I will need to tell myself that before I fully believe it.

"So," Rob says after a while, his eyes sparkling as he grins at me. "How about that early night then?"

This is it. The moment I have to decide whether I want to go through with this or not. I don't think I do. I mean yeah, Rob is good looking, funny, and I do kind of like him. But I just wanted to have a few drinks and enjoy myself, nothing more. If I say no now though, Blake will think it's because of him and I really don't want to give him the satisfaction of thinking he's influenced me at all.

I'm still debating what to say in answer to Rob's question when Blake speaks up. He keeps looking straight ahead, but it's obvious his words are directed at Rob.

"I don't think that's such a good idea. This is a business convention, not a night out," he says.

"Blake," I gasp, annoyed at his sheer audacity.

He must know that people hook up regularly at these conferences. Hell that's the attraction to attending the thing to a lot of the attendees.

"What?" Blake says, finally turning to look at me. "Would you have even been considering doing this if your father was with you? I just think you should show me the same level of respect that you show him, that's all."

"That's completely different and you know it," I snap.

"You know what?" Rob says, reminding me that he's still there, still waiting for my answer. I turn back to him as he stands up. "You're a great girl Kerry, but to be honest, I don't need all of this drama. I'm just looking for a bit of fun, nothing more, and this is getting way past that."

"Rob, wait," I say as Rob starts to walk away.

He doesn't wait. He doesn't even look back. He moves deeper into the room which is a lot more crowded now, moving away from me and looking for an easier target presumably. I guess I should think of this as a lucky escape, but I don't. It's not like I was looking for a relationship or anything, but if I was, Blake could have just ruined it completely for me.

"You are an absolute asshole," I snap to Blake.

I stand up and storm away, moving out of the bar and back across the lobby. I can hear Blake calling after me, but I have nothing to say to him. At least not here. I can feel anger swirling inside of myself and I am not about to embarrass myself by yelling at Blake here in front of the reception desk.

I head for the stairs, but as I pass the elevators, one of them stands open and empty and I veer towards it and get in. I press the button for the second floor and the doors start to shut. Before they can meet, a hand snakes in between them, stopping them from meeting and they spring wide open again. Blake steps into the elevator.

I debate stepping out, but I won't give him the satisfaction of changing my plans because of his actions and I stay in place, staring at the doors which are closing again. They close with a quiet bumping sound and then the elevator begins to move.

"Kerry," Blake says.

I ignore him and he grabs my hand and I turn to look at him, pulling my hand away from him. I don't get it clear before I feel the tingles spreading out and running up my arm from where he touched me. I swallow hard and look at him.

"Relax Kerry," Blake says with a smile. "Why are you so mad at me?"

His smile and his question does nothing to make the anger inside of me fade.

"Are you kidding me? Why the hell do you think I'm so mad at you?" I demand.

Blake shrugs his shoulders.

"I have no idea. Because if you really wanted to be with Rob right now and not me, you'd have gone running after him and told him what a douche bag I am," he says.

"That's why I'm mad at you," I shout. "I'm mad at you because you act like a prick all of the time and yet I still find myself wanting you. Are you happy now?"

I didn't mean to tell him everything like that. It just came out. To be honest, I didn't realize myself that's why I am so angry until I said it. I can feel the heat rushing into my cheeks and I think about trying to take the words back, but what's the point of that? Blake heard them loud and clear and stuttering and spluttering and trying to take them back is only going to make it even worse.

"Yes. I'm happy now," Blake says.

I open my mouth to tell him to go to hell, but I can't get the words out because his lips have closed over mine, his hands on my hips. I start to pull back, but at the last minute, I stop myself, because the truth is, I don't want to pull back. I want this to happen more than I've ever wanted anything to happen in my life.

BLAKE

B^{lake}

I didn't plan on kissing Kerry in the elevator. To be honest, I didn't plan on kissing Kerry at all really. I mean I wanted to kiss her more than anything, but I still didn't plan on actually doing it. I didn't think she would welcome my kiss. But then she went and admitted that she wanted me, and even if she was angry and yelling it at me, it was what I wanted to hear, and before I could talk myself out of it, my lips were on hers. If I had taken even a moment to think it through, I most likely wouldn't have had the courage to actually do it. For that reason, I'm glad I didn't let myself stop to think about it.

At first, Kerry tried to pull back from me when my lips found hers. I pushed a hand into her hair, stopping her from moving her mouth away from mine. Now I had finally tasted her, I couldn't bear the kiss to be over so soon, but I have to admit that I wondered for a moment if that was really a good idea or if it would make her feel afraid, like I was forcing her to do something she didn't want to do. I almost laughed at that thought. As if anyone could ever force Kerry Morgan to do anything she didn't want to do. There would be more chance of taming a lion.

As I debate releasing my grip on Kerry, I realize that she's kissing me back. She's no longer trying to pull back from me. Instead, she's doing the exact opposite of trying to pull away from me. She's pressing her body against mine. Her kiss is soft and gentle at first, like she's just testing the water, but within seconds it's a hungry, passionate kiss that sets my soul on fire and makes my cock rock hard.

Kerry's mouth tastes of wine and something sweet, something that I think is essentially her own taste, and I push my tongue deeper into her mouth, wanting to taste every part of her tongue, every part of her mouth. I run my hands up and down her back and over her hips and her ass. I want to feel every inch of her body beneath my fingers. I want to caress every inch of her body until she's begging me for more.

She is still pressing herself tightly against me and I can feel her breasts against my chest, her nipples hard and inviting against me. I want to drag her dress off her, rip her panties off her and fuck the life out of her right here, right now.

Even as I think about it, the elevator car lurches to a stop and makes a loud pinging sound as the doors open onto our floor. Kerry and I jump apart as though we've been burned, just waiting to be judged for acting like two horny teenagers in a public place, but we're ok, the corridor is deserted.

I don't say anything as we step out of the elevator car, afraid that I might break this delicious spell that's fallen over us if I speak up now. It seems as though Kerry feels the exact same way, because she doesn't speak either. She glances up at me, her eyes heavy with lust and then she looks away, facing straight ahead again. I reach down and take her hand in mine and lead her quickly along the corridor to our room. I fish out my key card with the hand not holding Kerry's hand, and I get our room door open. I pull Kerry inside and turn to face her as the door shuts behind us. The key card drops from my hand, landing on the ground, forgotten for now.

For a moment, Kerry and I stand there just looking at each other, our eyes flitting from each other's mouth to our eyes and back again, our chests heaving, and then we both move as one, coming back together, our lips finding each other, our hands roaming over each other's bodies.

Heat floods through my body and I reach down and grab the hem of Kerry's dress. I lift it up towards her head and she steps back from me for long enough for me to pull it over her head. She raises her arms and the dress is clear of her body. I toss it to the ground and then I look at Kerry. I get a brief flash of her skin, tanned and sleek, her black lacy underwear breaking the view up, and then we're kissing again and I'm kicking Kerry's dress away from us so we don't trip over it and I'm pushing her backwards, moving her against the door of the room.

When her back is against the door, I run my fingers down her arms and catch her wrists. I pull her arms up into the air above her head and bring her hands together. I wrap one hand around both of her wrists, keeping her hands in place, keeping her arms taut, her body pinned beneath my touch. I run the fingers of my spare hand down Kerry's arm and over her chest, down her stomach.

I pull my mouth from hers and kiss her neck as I push my hand into her panties and push my fingers between her lips, finding her clit. She is already wet, warm and slippery, and I moan with her as my fingers rub across her wet clit.

I move my head back, watching Kerry's reaction to me as I work her clit, her hands still held in place above her head. She looks amazing, her back arched, the tendons in her neck standing out, her breath coming in little gasps as she nears her orgasm. Her eyes are closed as she rides on the waves of pleasure. Her mouth drops open a little bit and she runs her tongue over her lips, sending another wave of red hot desire cascading through my body. She's so fucking sexy.

I apply more pressure on Kerry's soaking clit, speeding up my fingers, working her faster, moving her closer and closer to coming. I can feel her clit pulsing against my fingers as I rub her and I wait until I know she's right about to come, and then I pull my fingers out of her panties. Her eyes fly open, her mouth closing abruptly and she frowns at me. I ignore the frown and I smile at her, letting her know I'm just teasing her, that this night is far from over.

I release Kerry's hands and bring my arm down, and I pull her into my arms and kiss her hard on the mouth. My hands move over Kerry's lower back and then settle on her ass cheeks. She wraps her arms around my shoulders, kissing me back as deeply as I am kissing her, grinding her body against mine, one hand pushing up into my hair, pushing my lips even tighter against hers.

I turn, keeping Kerry held tightly in my arms and I walk her towards the bed in the middle of the room. I feel her legs bump against the bed and I stop for a moment. I move my hands up her back and unhook her bra, freeing her large breasts. I push her panties down her legs and she steps out of them and then I move back and her bra tumbles down her arms and joins her panties on the ground. Kerry stands before me fully naked now, her skin flushed pink and covered in a layer of sweat.

My breath catches in my throat as I look at this vision of beauty before me, and I know that no matter what has happened between us in the past, it's all been leading us to this moment. When I look at Kerry, I see a beautiful woman that is mine. I know now why I felt the surge of jealousy downstairs in the bar when I saw Kerry flirting with Rob. It's because as much as I try not to, I do already think of her as mine. I need to take tonight to show Kerry how good we can be together, because I have no intentions of letting her go again.

As I stand and study Kerry's amazing body, she gives me a sexy half smile and then she reaches out and grabs the bottom of my t-shirt, pulling it up and over my head. She fumbles my jeans open and pushes them down my legs. I kick my shoes off and then my jeans with them. My boxer shorts follow quickly behind and then I whip up each foot in turn and peel my socks off. Kerry and I are both completely naked now, facing each other, desperate for each other. I feel like I can smell Kerry's lust on the air, a thick exotic smell that makes me think of primal sex and heady orgasms.

My cock is pulsing as I look at Kerry's heaving chest, and I can't wait any longer before I can touch her again. I reach out and push her gently back onto the bed. She lands on her ass and she scoops backwards, laying down in the center of the mattress, inviting me to lay with her, her legs open, eager to receive me. I stand where I am for a moment, looking down at Kerry's glistening slit. I almost climax right there just looking at how wet she is, how swollen. She is that way because of me. It's good to know that I am affecting her body equally as much as she is affecting mine.

I swallow hard, forcing myself to hold myself back from coming now, keeping myself from ending this night before it's really begun, and then I get onto the bed, kneeling between Kerry's knees. She reaches for me and pulls me down on top of her. I let her lead me into place, holding my weight on my elbows at either side of her body.

I lean down and rub my lips against hers, a feather light, teasing touch, that makes Kerry moan. I kiss her again, and this time, there's nothing in the least bit gentle about it. I kiss her like I have never kissed anyone before, like I want that single kiss to be able to let her know how much I want this, how much I want her.

I kiss Kerry deeply and then I start to move my lips, kissing over her chin and down her neck. I kiss down her breast bone and I move to her right breast, kissing over it and then sucking the already hard nipple into my mouth. I swirl my tongue around it, loving the sound of her breath catching in her throat as I turn her on with my tongue. I release the nipple from my mouth, watching it pucker as the cool air washes over it. It still glistens, moist from my mouth.

I kiss across Kerry's chest and suck her other nipple into my mouth, giving it the same treatment as the first one, making her writhe beneath me. I can feel the heat from her pussy coming off her in waves, heating me and giving me a hint of what's to come when I finally allow myself to plunge into her warm and inviting depths. When I release her second nipple from my mouth, I run my tongue lightly over it and then I nip it between my teeth, making her cry out in surprise. Her cry cuts off, turning to a moan as I lick over the bite, soothing it.

I smile to myself as I resume my journey down Kerry's body, kissing my way down her belly. I feel her tense slightly as I move lower, anticipating what's to come, but she's wrong. I want her to wait a bit longer, to be really ready for this. I skip past her pussy even though it's hard to ignore it, and I shuffle backwards on the bed, running my tongue down her left inner thigh and then moving to her other leg and running my tongue up that inner thigh. She moans and gasps beneath me, more than ready for me to give her some release.

I am teasing myself almost as much as I am teasing Kerry. As I lick my way up her thigh, I can smell the musky scent of her lust, and I imagine the taste of her on my tongue, salt and sweetness together. I moan as I lift my head and shuffle closer to her pussy.

I lay on my belly and push Kerry's legs further apart, looking at her red, swollen slit. I run my tongue from her pussy to her clit and she cries out as I press down on her clit with the end of my tongue. I begin to lick her from side to side and she wraps her legs around my shoulders, pulling me tightly against her mound.

I can taste her, smell her, feel her juices coating my lips, my tongue, my face. It's like she's getting into every pore of my body, consuming each of my senses. It feels perfect, like we are becoming one with each other. I keep licking her. She's so close to her orgasm now. I can feel her clit pulsing beneath my tongue and I can hear her gasping breaths beneath the lapping sounds of me licking her.

I press down firmly with the tip of my tongue for a moment, and then I suck Kerry's sensitive clit into my mouth, squeezing it between my lips and running my tongue over it. I release it again and lick once more, licking harder and faster, ignoring the cramp that threatens my tongue.

Kerry's thighs tighten around me, holding me so tightly against her I can barely breath. Her hands are in my hair, pulling hard on fist fulls of it as she lifts her upper body from the mattress. She screams my name and then she's silent, not even breathing, her body rigid as her pussy tightens and then floods my face with a gush of warm juices.

Finally, she relaxes, her muscles quivering as her body flops back down onto the mattress. I move back from her pussy slightly as her thighs slip away from my shoulders and flop down onto the mattress on either side of me. We are both panting for air as I look at her wet pussy, and I imagine myself inside of her. My cock throbs just at the thought of it, and I know if I don't push myself inside of her soon, it'll be too late for me. I really can't resist her for much longer. I need to be inside of her right now.

KERRY

My heart is racing and I am gasping for breath as my orgasm begins to fade, leaving me tingly and relaxed and completely at one with my body. I have never had an orgasm like that before. It consumed me completely, spreading out through my whole body, each nerve tingling deliciously at once. My whole body went rigid and for a moment, I couldn't breathe, couldn't think. It was amazing. And that was before Blake and I even have sex. If he can do that with his tongue, I can only imagine what magic he can work on me with his cock.

I feel a little bit strange now, but good strange. Like I am a mixture of both fully sated and yet I'm also ready for more, hell I am desperate for more. I have had the most intense orgasm of my life, and it's just set me off wanting it more and more. I can't imagine a world where I no longer feel this good.

When Blake pushes himself up onto his hands and knees and crawls up over my body, I am more than ready to accept his kiss. He leans down, his face moving closer to mine, and our lips meet and I reach up, wrapping my arms around him, pulling him down on top of me once more. I can feel his hard cock pressing against my belly as he kisses me. It feels huge and I want to feel it inside of me now.

I reach down between us and wrap my fist around it, moving my hand up and down Blake's length. I was right about his cock feeling huge. It's long and fat and amazing and I know it will fill me all of the way up, make me feel amazing all over again. I can hardly wait for him to be inside of me.

Blake kisses my neck and across my shoulder as I work his cock. His breath comes in hot pants, blasts of heat moving over me, warming my skin again where his saliva cools it. He lets me play with his cock for a moment and then he reaches down and stops me, taking my wrist in his hand and pulling it away.

I know why he's done it; he's on the verge of coming and he wants to hold himself back. He wants to come inside of me. I want that too and I wait eagerly for him to fill me. Instead, he kisses me again, hard and full on the mouth and I feel my body melting into him, my mouth becoming one with his.

Blake moves his lips from mine and then he comes up onto his knees. He takes my hands and pulls me up into a sitting position and then we kiss again, a hungry kiss, a kiss so full of desperation and lust that it makes my pussy dribble, my juices running down my thighs leaving me feeling sticky.

Blake's hands roam over my back, sending trails of fire moving over my skin wherever he touches. I am in a constant state of lust, so ready to have him fill me and bring me to my climax once more. I lift myself off my ass and get to my knees and press myself against Blake. My body is touching his all of the way down the front, and once more, I can feel his hard cock against me. We stay in that position for a moment, both of us on our knees, our chests pressed together, our lips locked, and Blake's hands cupping my ass.

I start to push him backwards, wanting to get on top of him, but he has other ideas. He resists me pushing him backwards and he puts his hands on my hips, taking his mouth from mine and turning me. I work with him, turning until my back is against his front, my legs open and my calves on the outsides of his. He kisses my neck as I lean back against him and he runs one hand down my body and over my belly.

I can feel Blake's hard cock pressed against my ass cheek now as I writhe against him and he moans against my neck. His fingers move lower and then they're between my lips, working my clit, bringing me straight back to the edge. Blake works me until I am on the verge of coming, my whole body tingling, my breath coming in a series of gasps as my body pulses with need. And then he takes his fingers away, leaving me crying out in frustration.

Blake ignores my cry of protest, putting his hands on my shoulders and pushing me forwards. I get onto my hands and knees, my legs spread, my ass and pussy wide open, on show for him. He runs his fingers through my slit and then up through my ass crack, spreading my wetness all around and making me writhe. Next, he moves the tip of his cock through my slit, pressing it against my clit and then pulling it away, moving it back towards my opening.

Blake pauses, leaving his cock on my opening, moving his hips slightly so that his cock moves in a circular motion, teasing me. Just when I think I can't take this any longer, he grabs me by the hips and pulls me backwards, impaling me on his cock. I moan out loud as he fills me, stretching my pussy, making it his.

I go wild as he fills me, matching his thrusts move for move, pushing against my hands, throwing myself back against him, wanting to take every inch of his cock inside of me. Each thrust rubs his cock over my g-spot and I can feel my orgasm bubbling up inside of me again.

I reach up with one hand, shoving my fingers between my lips and work my clit frantically, moving my fingers in time with Blake's desperate thrusting. I can feel my whole body tingling, my clit and pussy pulsing. Liquid drenches me, running freely from my pussy and down my thighs.

My orgasm slams through me, sending fire trailing through my pussy, through my clit, and up into the depths of my stomach. It keeps spreading out, infiltrating my chest, my limbs. I can't breathe. My lungs are frozen, rigid, pulsing like the rest of my body. My mouth is open, gaping, gasping for air, but I can't get any.

I feel another blast of ecstasy spread through my body and my pussy clenches tightly, wrapping itself around Blake's cock like a glove. He calls out my name as I tighten around him, but he still keeps thrusting, holding his orgasm back for a little bit longer.

Another wave of pleasure hits me, spreading down my limbs, making me weak. My hand falls away from my clit as my elbows buckle and I fall face down on the bed. With a great effort, I turn my face to one side, laying on my cheek as Blake continues to pump into me, thrusting harder and faster, pulling my hips back to meet his thrusts.

He moans my name and then he goes rigid inside of me, his cock stills for a second, and then it twitches and he spurts into me, a rush of heat against my cervix. His hands lock on my hips, holding my ass against his body as he yells out my name once more and spurts again. He releases me and slips out of me, falling beside me on the mattress. I spread my legs out and we lay side by side, both of us gasping and panting like we'll never be able to breathe normally again.

After a few minutes of course, my breathing does start to return to normal and I roll over onto my side and fish the duvet out from beneath me, covering myself. Blake follows my lead and gets beneath the duvet beside me.

"I guess you're over the idea of wanting me to take the floor then?" I grin.

"Well you've already made a mess of the covers. You might as well stay in here now," he grins back.

I laugh and gently swat his arm. He kisses my forehead and then he closes his eyes and his breathing soon evens out and I realize he has fallen asleep. I can feel sleep creeping up on me too and with a contented sigh, I close my eyes and let myself fall asleep.

KERRY

I come awake slowly at first, swaddled by a lovely soft duvet. I remember where I am, and as soon as that memory comes back, I also remember exactly what happened last night. I instantly regret it. For all I remember how much I enjoyed it at the time – and I really did; I have to admit it was the best sex I have ever had – I know we can't let it happen again.

In the cold light of day, I am back to knowing that as much as I find Blake attractive physically and as fun as last night was, we're just not compatible. He doesn't like me as a person and I don't particularly like him as a person either. We're not suited to each other at all. Part of me wishes we were, and that part shouts up suddenly, asking me if I really dislike Blake that much that we couldn't find a way to work through that. Maybe we could, I don't know. But even if I thought that we could, that doesn't mean we can, because of the simple fact that I'm pretty sure Blake doesn't want us to be together. Last night will have to be the end of the road for us.

We've got it out of our system now and we will just go back to business as usual now.

I push the duvet back and sit up and then I get out of the bed. The room is warm enough but I feel goosebumps dancing over my skin anyway when I look back down at the bed and see Blake. He's still sleeping and so I take a moment to study him. He really is hot, and as much as the logical part of me is still reminding me that last night was a mistake and that it can't happen again, there's another part of me that is tempted to kiss him awake and have one last session before we have to go back to reality.

I decide against the idea. If I kiss Blake and he wakes up and regrets last night and pushes me away, I would never get over the shame of it. And if he doesn't, if he welcomes my kiss and we have sex again, I'm honestly not sure I could bear to let him go again. I have to be strong. I have to resist him, even though right now that feels like pretty much the hardest thing I've ever had to do.

I move quickly to the chest of drawers, looking away from Blake before I can change my mind and do something that will no doubt embarrass me. I open the second drawer down and dig out my clean underwear, then pull out my jeans and the pale pink t-shirt I've brought to travel home in. I close the drawer and start to go towards the bathroom when I spot my dirty underwear on the ground from last night. Blushing slightly, I scoop it up and shove it in the side pocket of my luggage. I'll put it away properly later when I pack.

I go into the bathroom and lock the door behind me. I use the toilet and brush my teeth and then I get into the shower. The water is lovely and hot this morning and I wonder if it's because it's so early that no one else has used much of it yet, or if it's just because I'm in a better mood than I was yesterday so today I am appreciating it more. I don't suppose it matters much one way or the other now.

I wash my hair and then I stand for a few minutes, letting the spray run over my face, washing away the traces of last night's makeup that still cling to my face. Finally, I switch the water off and step out of the shower. I wrap myself in one of the towels and then I sit down on the closed toilet lid and begin to apply fresh make up. I dry and style my hair and then I dry my body and get dressed. I collect all of my things up and take them back into the bedroom ready for when I need to pack.

I step back into the main bedroom, and my stomach swirls slightly when I see that Blake is awake now. He looks gorgeous, his hair a bit disheveled from sleep. He's sitting up in bed and he smiles at me a little bit sheepishly as I come into the room. I return the smile and walk around to my side of the bed and put my things down.

"You must have been up early," Blake says, nodding towards me. "You're already showered and dressed."

"Yeah, I woke up early and figured I might as well just get moving," I say.

"That's a shame," Blake says with a grin. "I was kind of looking forward to waking up beside you."

I feel the heat in my cheeks and I wonder for a moment if Blake means it. Could he really have wanted to wake up with me? No. Of course he didn't really want to. He's just teasing me. He has to be.

"About that Blake," I say, sitting down on the bed and facing Blake. "It can't happen again between us. What happened last night I mean. It... it was a mistake."

"Ok," he says.

He pushes the duvet back and I look away quickly before I realize he's put his boxer shorts back on. I still don't look back at him. I am too angry to even look at him right now as he stands up, his back to me. Of course I can't help looking back at him. He stretches, the muscles in his back pulling taut, and I curse myself for even noticing his muscles.

Blake turns back around and I look away quickly, concentrating on picking a piece of fluff off my knee. There is no fluff. I glance at Blake out of the corner of my eye, hoping he hadn't noticed me watching him. He had noticed. I know he had noticed. I guess I just hoped he would pretend like he hadn't noticed. I should have known better. He grins and I shake my head.

"What's funny?" I say.

"Nothing," Blake says. "I was just smiling at the way you're trying to say you don't want us to sleep together again, but at the same time, you can't stop yourself from looking at me while I'm practically naked."

"Oh get over yourself Blake," I grumble, embarrassed that he has sussed me out so completely and that he has so brazenly announced it like that.

"What's your problem Kerry? Jeez, I was only messing with you," Blake says, shaking his head.

"I don't have a problem," I mutter. "Now if you don't mind, I have to get packed."

Blake opens his mouth to speak but then he seems to think better of it and he closes his mouth again. He shakes his head, sighs loudly and then he heads for the bathroom. The door closes behind him and then I hear the shower go on and I punch the mattress, making a loud moan of frustration once I'm sure that Blake won't hear me over the sound of the running water.

God what the hell is wrong with me? I am the one who said that Blake and I sleeping together was a mistake. I am the one who said that it can't happen again between us. And then I am still the one who got angry when Blake agreed with me. I guess part of me thought he might try to persuade me otherwise. Or at least seem a bit upset by my revelation rather than just agree with me. Does his quick agreement mean he regrets it too? And even if it does mean that, does it matter? Isn't it better that we're both on the same page with this?

I punch the mattress again. Dammit, I'm losing my fucking mind here. And it's all Blake's fault. I don't know why I'm letting him affect me so damned much, but I am and it's driving me mad. Now I'm angry at myself for being angry with Blake. I am just a tightly wound little ball of anger and none of it is in the least bit justified. I know that is true, and yet I also know I won't apologize to Blake for snapping at him. I'm such an asshole. Maybe I'm the problem rather than Blake. Maybe I'm the one who is hard to get along with, because everyone is always telling me how nice Blake is all of the damned time.

By the time Blake comes back out of the bathroom, I have finished packing and I am ready to go. I have calmed down a little bit, but my embarrassment level is still pretty high and it only gets higher when I see Blake, naked except for a towel wrapped around his waist.

I look away quickly, not willing to be caught perving on Blake yet again. I shouldn't even want to be perving on him, not even a little bit, but fuck me I really do want to. He just looks so damned good all of the time. I want to go over to him and pull the towel away from him. I want to get down on my knees in front of him and suck his cock into my mouth. I want to suck him until he comes and then swallow down his delicious come. And then I want to fuck him senseless until he comes again, filling me with his heat. Oh I need him inside of me so badly.

"Um Kerry? Are you alright?" Blake asks.

I glance at him. He's looking at me in concern and I frown.

"I'm fine. Why wouldn't I be alright?" I gasp.

God it's like he can read my mind and he wants to go out of his way to embarrass me. Maybe I should have just told him what's troubling me, see if that would have stopped him in his tracks.

"You were almost hyperventilating," Blake says. "I figured that meant something might be wrong. Excuse me for caring."

I feel myself blushing and I'm so glad that I'm wearing foundation so Blake won't be able to see the deep red color I know I have turned. I stand up and move towards the window, pulling the curtains aside and looking outside.

"I'm just a little bit too hot that's all," I say.

"It is pretty hot in here," Blake says.

I glance back over my shoulder ready to bite his head off, but he's moving back into the bathroom with his clean boxer shorts and a pair of jeans in his hand and I realize he wasn't actually being sarcastic. He was genuinely agreeing with me. The room actually is a little bit too warm now I come to think about it.

I go back to the bed and pull the duvet straight and then I sit down on the edge of the bed with a sigh. I need to get my head together because this tip toeing around Blake is annoying me already. We had sex, we won't have sex again. That's all there is to it. I have to stop looking for hidden meanings in everything he says to me.

After a few minutes, Blake comes back out of the bathroom clothed from the waist down now and I try not to look at his bare chest. I allow myself to look at his bare back as he pulls a t-shirt from the chest of drawers and by the time he turns around trying to catch me in the act of ogling him no doubt, I have picked my cell phone up and I'm scrolling through my Instagram feed, spoiling his bit of fun. I wonder vaguely if Blake is disappointed that he didn't catch me watching him this time because he actually wants me to want him, or if he is just because he missed a chance to wind me up and try to embarrass me further. I tell myself it doesn't matter one way or the other.

Blake pulls the t-shirt on and then he moves around the room collecting up his things and stuffing them into his bag. When he's ready, he checks his watch.

"We have about half an hour before the car is due to collect us. Do you want to grab some breakfast?" he asks.

"Sure," I agree.

I am pretty hungry, and besides that, the idea of sitting in the room alone with Blake for the next half an hour is more than I can bear. The tension between us is palpable now and I am just waiting for something to erupt between us. At least if we're in public, we'll have to keep our clothes on which is both a blessing and a curse.

We head out of the room and before I pull the door closed behind me, I do a last sweep around to check that we haven't left anything behind. We haven't and we leave the room and go to the elevator. We head to the restaurant and choose a table and then we head up to the buffet breakfast. We both choose the full English and then we head back to the table and sit down, our luggage beside us.

"So do you want to talk about what happened or do you want things to stay awkward between us?" Blake asks.

"There's nothing to talk about," I say.

"Cool. Awkward it is then," Blake grins.

I sigh and shake my head, telling myself this is why I dislike Blake so much, and also telling myself not to let him get underneath my skin so easily. That's easier to think than it is to actually do though. He's so bloody irritating.

"Well what do you want to say about it?" I ask, trying to turn this around onto him.

"Nothing in particular," he says.

"You were the one who thought we needed to talk about it," I point out.

"I thought maybe you had something to say seeing as how you're the one who has been acting weird all morning," Blake says.

Dammit. I almost snap at him. It's my go to reaction whenever Blake and I talk, but I stop myself. Maybe he's right. Maybe we do need to talk about things and then we can go back to normal. Maybe we can even be a little bit less frosty with each other than we used to be. Because we still have a big project to work on together when we get back to the office, and this weird awkwardness between us is even worse than the obvious animosity towards each other that we normally display.

"I guess... well... I guess it is a little awkward between us now isn't it? With us still having to work together and everything," I say.

Blake shrugs his shoulders.

"It doesn't have to be. We're both adults Kerry. We both knew there was some chemistry between us so we chose to act on it and get it out of our systems. And now we did. We don't have to let that hang over us," Blake says.

Blake seems to be choosing his words very carefully, but if he's doing that to try and make things better between us, then he's doing a terrible job of it. I actually have to wonder if he's purposely trying to choose words he thinks will hurt me, but that's surely a step too far, even for Blake. It was his idea for us to talk about this after all, and he must know that we need to at least be able to be civil to each other for the sake of the development project.

"Right. So now it's out of our systems, we can just go back to hating each other. Is that what you're saying?" I say coldly, trying not to let him see that his words have pierced my armor.

"No, but the way you're going on, it sure seems like that's what you want," Blake says.

"Yeah? Well maybe it is," I reply.

"Then consider it done," Blake says.

"Fine," I agree.

We finish the rest of our breakfast in silence, the atmosphere between us now even more awkward than it was before we tried to clear the air. I don't know how things degenerate so quickly whenever Blake and I try to talk. He does rub me up the wrong way, and clearly I do the same thing to him, but I feel like there's a reason we keep going around in circles like this, more of a reason than us rubbing each other the wrong way.

I think for my part, it's because I'm so determined to show Blake I am not bothered by his reaction to our night together that I'm going too far and actually being nasty to him. And maybe it's possible he's doing the exact same thing. Or maybe that's just wishful thinking on my part. Maybe he really does regret our night together and he was relieved when I said I didn't want it to happen again, and now he just can't fathom out what my problem is.

I can barely fathom out what my problem is lately. As always, it all seems to come back to Blake, but this time, instead of it stemming from the fact I hate him, it's stemming from the fact that maybe, just maybe, I don't hate him half as much as I wish I could right now.

~

I can't believe it's Monday morning already. Despite the issues Blake and I have with each other, the weekend with him flew over. Even the stonily silent plane ride home from the conference went by quickly enough. And of course the rest of Sunday flew by as Sundays always seem to when you're just relaxing and having a movie day. I think the fact I was kind of dreading Monday morning made Sunday fly past way faster too.

I came into work early today, wanting to get into my office before Blake arrived so there was no chance of me running into him in the parking lot or anywhere. I know that I'm obviously going to have to see Blake eventually, especially now we're working so closely together, but that's different. I'll be prepared for that. It would be so much worse to just run into him unexpectedly. I want to be cool and calm and professional when I do have to face him, not flustered and stuttering like I would be if it was a chance encounter that I wasn't ready for.

A knock sounds on my office door and I cringe a little bit before I look up and see it's not Blake. It's only Lisa peering through my little window. I relax and smile, beckoning for her to come in. She comes into my office and closes the door and comes and sits down on the other side of my desk.

"Well look at you all keen for work," she laughs. "I didn't think I'd ever see the day you actually beat me into the office."

"You make it sound like I'm usually late," I laugh back.

"I didn't mean it like that," Lisa says. "Honestly, I'm just winding you up. Seriously though, I am a little bit shocked that you're in so early today. I thought you would have taken a half day after the conference like you usually do."

I shake my head.

"No, not this time," I say.

Lisa raises an eyebrow at me but she doesn't press me for the reason behind my decision, although I know we'll most likely end up circling back to it and when we do, I know I'll end up telling her what's going on. I did think about taking my usual half day Monday that I've always taken after the conference, but I knew that meant I had a higher chance of running into Blake as I made my way through the building. I have to pass his office to get to mine, and I wasn't confident I could time it to make the dash past when he was having his lunch break or something.

"So how did the conference go?" Lisa asks.

"Good," I say. "I enjoyed it. It's always nice to catch up with everyone, and there were some really good speakers this year too."

I run through a few of the key points from some of the talks I attended to illustrate my point about the conference having really good speakers this year and Lisa oohs and aahs in all of the right places. I'm sure she's as impressed by the key points as I was. After I tell her the useful stuff, I tell her about the funny keynote speech and then I tell her all about the issues with our hotel room.

"Oh my God, you and Blake had to share a room?" Lisa exclaims. "So while the conference itself went well, the weekend wasn't quite what you expected."

I cringe inside. I hadn't thought through the fact that me telling her about the screw up with the rooms would inevitably lead to her working out that Blake and I had indeed had to resort to sharing a room. I grimace and nod.

"Yup," I say. "We had to share a room. And to say that wasn't what I signed up for with this thing is an understatement."

"Oh that must have been fun," Lisa laughs.

"Fun. Yeah. That's one word for it," I smile. "I did meet a guy who almost saved me from my fate though."

That should help to move the conversation on from Blake and our close proximity.

"Ooh tell me more," Lisa says, leaning forward, her elbows resting on my desk, her chin on her palms.

"His name was Rob. He was cute. He was tall, and he had this thick blonde hair, and he had really nice eyes. We clicked and we were having a laugh, but then Blake turned up and spoilt everything. He kept making sarcastic comments, and in the end, Rob decided he didn't need the drama," I say. "And who can blame him? Generally speaking, the whole point of a one night stand is that there's no mess and no drama involved right?"

"Right. I wouldn't fancy having been Blake when you got done with him after that one," Lisa laughs.

"We slept together," I blurt out.

I can't believe I've gone from trying to divert the conversation away from Blake and I to blurting out the truth just like that without Lisa even asking about it.

"Well yeah, you had to didn't you because of the screw up. But I bet you gave him a right ear ache after he scared Rob away," she says. "You must have gone to town on him right?"

"No Lisa, you don't understand. We slept together slept together," I say.

"What do you...? Ohhh. I see," Lisa said. "Well shit. I so did not see that one coming. Murder maybe. Sex. No way."

She shakes her head and grins at me.

"You're a right dark horse Kerry," she says, her eyes sparkling as she leans closer to me. "So how was it?"

"Honestly Lisa, it was the most amazing sex I've ever had in my life. I had orgasms like the ones people talk about in romance books. The ones that we always think are just made up," I say with a sigh of pleasure as I remember just how good Blake and I were together.

"Angry hate sex is obviously your thing," Lisa states with a soft laugh.

"Yeah, maybe it is," I say. "If hating people can make it be like that, then screw love. I'm going on a mission to hate any guy I might date."

We both laugh at that although I'm not entirely joking.

"So what happens now then? With you and Blake?" Lisa asks. "More hot angry hate sex or are you actually going to date each other?"

"Neither. There is no me and Blake. What happened was amazing in the moment, but it was a mistake and we need to move past it," I say.

"Did he buy that? Because I'm as sure as hell not buying it for even one little second. You're smitten with him," Lisa laughs. "You're just that used to saying you hate him, it's like your default mode now."

"I… yeah, he bought it," I say, deciding against even trying to lie to Lisa about how much of a mess I made of everything. "I told Blake the next morning that what we did was a mistake and that it couldn't happen again. I sort of meant it, but if I'm being honest, there was a part of me that hoped he would say that it wasn't a mistake at all, and that he would take me in his arms and kiss away my objections."

"And I'm assuming that's not what happened then?" Lisa says.

"Nope. He just casually accepted it," I say.

Lisa laughs and I frown.

"What's funny?" I ask.

"You are," she says, shaking her head. "You got pissed off at him for agreeing with you didn't you?"

I nod sheepishly.

"Yeah. I guess maybe I just wanted it to have meant something to him," I say.

"Well maybe it did. I mean it clearly meant something to you but you pretended it was a mistake. What's to say Blake isn't doing the same thing?" Lisa says.

"Why would he lie about it?" I demand.

"Well I don't know. Why did you lie about it?" Lisa says.

"To save face I suppose. I figured Blake would regret what we had done, so I thought I would get in first and say I regretted it. And that's what I did, and obviously I was right and Blake did regret it," I say.

"Or you were totally wrong and Blake just didn't feel the need to beg you to have sex with him again," Lisa says.

I can't help but remember what Blake said to me about wanting to have woken up with me. And then the way he laughed when he caught me looking at him half naked. Surely that wasn't the action of someone who regretted sleeping with me.

"Maybe," I concede. "It would have been nice if he had been willing to fight for me a little bit though. And that's Blake isn't it? What he wants, he gets. So if he wanted me, he wouldn't have held back from just saying that."

I realize I am talking myself in and out of the idea of Blake possibly wanting us to hook up again, and I am changing my mind mid-sentence. Lisa can keep up though. We've been best friends for long enough for her to know about the way I jump through ideas this way. She is usually the voice of reason, and it looks like this time is going to be no exception.

"Do you want to know what I think?" Lisa asks me, looking thoughtful.

"Does it matter what I say to that or are you going to tell me anyway?" I grin.

"Oh I'm going to tell you anyway," Lisa says with a laugh. "But it would be nice to know you actually care what I think."

"Ok, hit me with it," I say.

"I think you should give Blake a chance. Stop resisting these feelings so much. You've become so obsessed with the idea of hating Blake that you can't see that there's really no need for it," Lisa says.

I open my mouth to argue with her, to tell her that she's crazy and it's not like that at all, but I stop myself and actually think about what she has said. Could it be true? Could I just be assuming that I still hate Blake because it's been my go to stance on him for so long?

"It's too late," I say sadly, shaking my head. "Even if you're right about me clinging to an old notion – and I'm not saying you are; I'm just saying that there's a tiny chance that you might be – Blake hates me even more than ever now."

"What makes you say that?" Lisa asks me.

I shrug my shoulders.

"Everything," I sigh. I pause for a moment and then I go on. "Let's just say I wasn't exactly a ray of sunshine on this trip. I was hungover and every little thing pissed me off and I didn't exactly hold back from making that known."

"Well clearly he got over that enough to have sex with you, so it's not all bad," Lisa says.

We both laugh at that. Lisa stands up after a moment.

"Well I'd better go and get some work done," she says. "Think about what I said ok? Give Blake a chance. Sure you might end up regretting it, but I honestly think you'll end up regretting it more if you don't give him a chance."

I smile and nod in agreement. I don't know whether she's right or not, and I don't know whether it's a good idea to come around to the idea of giving Blake a chance, but I will definitely think about it. Not right now though. Right now, I need to go and talk to Sasha and find out what the hell happened with our hotel room booking. She should be in by now.

I let Lisa get out of sight first. I don't want to embarrass Sasha in front of anyone. She's always been a good assistant and this will really be the first mistake I've ever known her to make. I just want to give her a head's up to make sure nothing like that ever happens again, rather than yell at her, and that's even assuming that it's her fault. There's still a good possibility in my mind that the hotel is the ones who fucked up the booking.

I wander out of my office and go to Sasha's desk. She looks up and smiles when she sees me approaching.

"Good morning," she says.

"Good morning," I reply.

"How was the conference?" Sasha asks, still smiling.

"It was fine except for a problem with the hotel room booking. That's actually what I wanted to talk to you about," I say.

Sasha cringes and shakes her head.

"Shit. I'm sorry Kerry. I knew I should have handled it myself but I was swamped and Annette said she would take care of the hotel room reservations. I should have said no, I almost did, but..."

"Wait, are you saying that Annette did the booking?" I interrupt her.

Sasha nods her head, looking a bit sheepish. I smile at her.

"Relax Sasha, I'm not annoyed about that," I say. "I just want to get to the bottom of it. We ended up with one of our rooms being cancelled and I'm just trying to work out if it's really a mistake at this end like the hotel is claiming it is, or if it's a mistake at their end like I believe it's more likely to be."

"Oh right," Sasha says. "Well I can't see how Annette would have somehow managed to accidentally cancel one of the rooms. I'd guess it was a glitch at the hotel's end too."

I nod.

"It sure seems that way. Anyway, I'll go and talk to Annette. I don't want to call the hotel and cause a scene and then find out it actually is a mistake at our end," I say.

"Oh yeah, that would be so embarrassing," Sasha says. "Do you want me to find Annette and have her come to your office?"

"No it's ok. I'll go to her. I need to stretch my legs anyway," I smile.

Sasha nods her head and I walk away as she goes back to her work. I don't really need to stretch my legs, but I think if Annette has made a mistake, she'll be more likely to admit it if I go to her. If she is summoned to my office, she's more likely to think she is in trouble and try to hide it. Now I am no longer hungover, I don't want to tear Annette a new one, I just want to make sure this doesn't happen again, whoever made the mistake.

I walk through the office and find Annette at her desk on the phone. I sit down on the edge of her desk and wait for her to finish talking. She ends the call and looks up at me.

"Is everything ok?" she asks me.

"Sasha said you had offered to make our hotel room reservations for the conference for her," I start.

Annette nods her head.

"I did. Was that a problem? Just she was swamped and I was waiting for a client who was running late so I thought I would help her out," she tells me.

"It's fine," I say. "But when we got there, we found out that one of the rooms was cancelled. They tried to blame us, but I reckon it's their mistake so I'm just trying to get to the bottom of it all."

Annette's face crumples and she gasps.

"Oh God Kerry, I'm so sorry. I think it was my fault," she says. "I made the booking and then I realized you wanted a room with a balcony and I hadn't booked one with a balcony. I called to change one of the rooms to one with a balcony but I must have messed it up and cancelled the room altogether."

Annette looks really upset as she looks up at me and I realize she's waiting for me to yell at her. Annette has made a mistake and so I can understand why she thinks she'll be in trouble.

It doesn't seem fair though having a go at her for trying to help Sasha when she was so busy and I don't want to make her any more upset than she already looks. I reach out and squeeze her shoulder.

"Hey don't look so worried," I say. "It's not a big deal."

"It is though. I messed up," she says.

"Look I only wanted to get to the bottom of this because I wanted to be sure it wasn't our mistake before I called the hotel about it. Now I know it is our mistake, I won't call so your honesty has saved me from looking stupid. Honestly it was an easy enough mistake to make Annette. Don't sweat it ok?" I say.

Annette smiles gratefully at me and I squeeze her shoulder again as I get up off her desk and head back to my office. I'm glad I decided to talk to Sasha before I called the hotel and made a scene. I would have been forced to eat humble pie if I had called them straight away like I was tempted to do.

It's time to let this go and start worrying about something more important. Something like the reports we need for the new development. Reports I will be generating alone because the thought of running into Blake right now is making my stomach churn and I want to be able to concentrate on getting the reports right, something I doubt I could do with Blake around me distracting me with his hotness.

BLAKE

It's been a couple of days since Kerry and I came back from the conference. That means it's also been a couple of days since I finally admitted to myself that I was into Kerry despite her bitching and moaning. I have thought of nothing but her since that night. Somehow, us having sex sealed the deal for me and made me want her even more. I feel like that night has only made me even more into her, where for her, it seems that she really did get any attraction she felt for me out of her system and that we're done with all of it now.

I have spent years telling myself that I hate that damned girl, and now I have finally realized that I was wrong and I definitely don't hate her – in fact it's the total opposite of that for me - it makes no difference because I've already fucked up any chance I might have had with her.

Honestly, being around the office and catching glimpses of her, hearing her voice, it is driving me totally crazy. I feel like I am losing my mind being so close to Kerry but not being able to have her. Not being able to hold her or to kiss her or even being able to talk to her.

I know there's no chance of Kerry and I being together again, not even just for one more night of insane pleasure. Kerry hates me now more than ever. She won't even look at me now, let alone anything else. I kind of hoped that there was a chance she would feel the same way about me as I feel about her. That the night we spent together would have shown her just how good we could be together as well, but it seems that it's done the opposite for her at least.

Maybe if I could just get her to talk to me, she would come around and see that I'm not so bad, and that would be the first step to her seeing that actually, we'd be good together. Suddenly the project we're working on together doesn't seem like a punishment anymore. It feels like a god send, because there's no way she can ignore me when we're doing work on the same thing like that. She might still keep it cool and professional, but it's something that gives me an excuse to be around her without looking like a crazy person or like I am desperate, and it's my chance to show her that I'm really not a total douche bag.

I think for a moment, wondering if there's any way to make this project move a little bit faster so that Kerry and I can be drawn together sooner. An idea comes to me and I smile to myself and then I lift up the telephone and make a call.

I am smiling to myself even more when the call is over. I punch the air in delight and then I turn to my computer and fire off an email to Kerry. An email informing her that I've just spoken to the head of the shareholders and several of the board members want to come in and hear where we are so far on the new development project.

I refrain from telling Kerry that the meeting was my idea. She doesn't need to know that part. All she needs to know is that we're having this meeting. And once the shareholders leave, maybe we will get a chance to actually talk to each other. It's worth doing a presentation to the shareholders to get a chance at that.

As I sit thinking about the possibility of Kerry and I actually having a conversation again, a conversation we can have alone once the shareholders leave the office, an email pings into my inbox and my heart skips a beat when I see that it's from Kerry.

I open the email and read it quickly. It's short and to the point, asking me simply when and where the meeting will be held, but I still get a rush of goosebumps over me as I hear the questions in Kerry's voice in my head. This is the first time that Kerry has spoken to me - electronically or other-wise - since we got back from the conference and it might be a quick-communication, but I'll take it. It means we're on the right path, because if she was determined not to speak to me at all, she would have called my assistant for the time and place of the meeting.

I type out a reply to Kerry letting her know that the meeting will be in the conference room tomorrow afternoon at two o'clock and then I start putting the finishing touches to some of the reports I will have to present.

It's hard to concentrate on anything but Kerry, but I force myself to push her out of my mind for the moment, telling myself that tomorrow will have to be soon enough for her to consume me once more.

KERRY

I check the time and see that I have half an hour to go before the meeting with the shareholders is due to start. The presentation for them is all done and it's saved to my laptop ready to pull up once my laptop is synced to the screen in the conference room. I have checked and double checked it and I know it's right. I know it's promising too, the kind of thing that is going to make the shareholders sit up and take notice. This development is going to make them all very happy because if we pull it off, and there's no reason to think we won't do that, then it's going to make them all very rich.

The more I think about the presentation and the project, the more excited I get. It's a big one, and I can feel it deep inside of myself that it is going to become something very special indeed. It's the sort of feeling I have only had twice before, and both of those times, I was right about the projects being amongst the best investments the firm had ever made and I really think this one is going to top the last two put together.

The houses are going to be amazing and we are going to have buyers clambering to buy them all. I just know it.

My excitement turns to a nervous flutter inside of me, and I am tempted to open the presentation and go through it once more but I resist the urge. I know that I've entered the right information from my own reports and from the ones that Blake sent over to me first thing this morning. The only thing that has changed since the last time I checked the report is that I've had lunch, and I don't really think that is relevant to the shareholders.

I don't really want to go into the presentation now if I can avoid it because it's on the right page to start. I hate it when I'm in a meeting and someone else is doing a presentation and they have to scroll around to find their start place before they can begin. I've got this and I know I have and I just have to find something else to do for a little while to stop the nervous feeling inside of me.

I debate going to the conference room now and getting myself set up and settled, but I decide against it. If Blake has also decided to be a little bit early for the meeting, then we'll end up alone in the conference room together and the thought of that half an hour of awkwardness isn't something I want or need right now. Instead, I turn to my computer and go to my email – there's bound to be something there that requires my attention and can stop me thinking about this.

I am soon engrossed in my inbox, and I just have time to deal with a few queries and then it's finally time to head to the conference room. I take a deep breath and then I grab my laptop and leave my office.

I reach the conference room and find it empty and I instantly kick myself for not coming along earlier like I wanted to. Blake never comes early for meetings – he says it makes it look as though he has nothing better to do and that gives the wrong impression, especially to shareholders who think time is money.

I sigh and shake my head at myself for not remembering that sooner, and then I busy myself setting up the room. I close down my email and open up the title page of our presentation and then I hook my laptop up to the screen that I pull down. I smile in satisfaction when the screen displays my laptop's screen as I had planned. As I step away from the screen and move to the refreshment area to make sure everything is in order, the door opens behind me.

I am instantly aware of Blake in the room with me. I can smell his aftershave and the musky hint of him beneath it. My temperature goes up a couple of degrees and my breath catches in my throat as I feel his presence behind me. My pussy clenches longingly and I can feel myself getting wet. I wish we didn't have to have a meeting. That instead, he was here for me. I can imagine him coming up behind me, his hands roaming over my body...

"Good afternoon," Blake says, breaking me out of my momentary fantasy.

I turn to face him, hoping my face isn't as red as it feels. I thought I was prepared to come face to face with Blake, but I realize now that I'm not. Not even a little bit. My body responds to the sight of him, my clit tingling and my nipples hardening. I swallow hard, trying to swallow down the desire that floods me when I look at Blake. I want to hate him, but my body has other ideas and for now at least, my body is winning the battle.

"Good afternoon," I say breezily, glad that my voice doesn't betray me even if the flush of my cheeks probably already has. "Everything seems to be in order."

"Good," Blake says. If he has noticed my discomfort, he is doing a good job of ignoring it. "The shareholders will be starting to arrive at any moment."

I nod and turn back to the refreshments table and pour myself a coffee. I grudgingly pour one for Blake and turn back and hand it to him without bothering to ask him if he wants it or not. He takes it and thanks me and we go and sit down at the conference room table. Blake pulls his cell phone out and engrosses himself in it and I wish I had thought to bring mine, but I didn't and I am stuck sipping my coffee as my only distraction.

Luckily, I don't have long to wait before the shareholders start to trickle in. Blake puts his cell phone away and we begin to greet each shareholder as they enter and then make polite conversation with them until they have all arrived and are seated.

"Well. Should we get started then?" I ask when everyone is seated and everyone that said yes to refreshments has a drink in front of them.

My request is met by a series of nods and yeses and I stand up and move to the front of the room to stand beside my laptop. I feel a swirl of butterflies in my tummy and my mouth feels dry, but as I click into the presentation and begin to speak, my nerves melt away.

As I talk, I can feel Blake's eyes on me. All of the eyes in the room are on me, but none of them feel like Blake's do. None of them cut through my skin and see into my very soul. But with my nerves gone and my confidence soaring, Blake's gaze doesn't distract me. In fact, it encourages me, pushing me on, and I know my presentation is better than I could have even dared to hope it would be. And something in Blake's eyes tells me that he doesn't regret sleeping with me anymore than I regret sleeping with him.

My part of the presentation finally ends to polite applause and nods of approval. I smile my thanks, and then I pause the presentation on my laptop to take questions. I get asked a few questions, but it's nothing I can't handle and I answer them quickly and fully. The shareholders are nodding approvingly to each other again by the time I take my seat and Blake stands up to do his part of the presentation. I watch him as he starts to talk and soon enough, he has warmed up and he has the shareholders as captivated as I did. And yes, I admit it - he has me captivated too.

He paces about as he talks, but it's not a nervous pacing, it's an assured movement, a sinewy show of muscle and grace. Now and again as Blake talks, he gestures with his hands and each time one of his hands moves, I picture him moving closer to me and putting one of those hands on my body. I imagine the heat from his palm, the pleasure coasting through me, brought on by his touch and it is starting to become harder and harder to keep my composure. I know my cheeks are flushed and my pussy is dripping wet; it's all I can do to sit in my seat without wriggling. I swallow and look away from Blake for a moment, trying to bring myself back to the present moment.

I just about manage to get myself under control and I look back up and I bite my lip, holding back a smile as I watch Blake shine. He turns and hits the arrow button on my laptop, moving the presentation forward and displaying the next screen. Horror fills me as soon as the next screen displays. The figures are wrong. I can see it from here, without even having to think about it. Blake is still talking, oblivious to the glaring error behind him. I should speak up, warn him, but I am frozen and I find myself mute. The shareholders begin to look at each other with frowns, each wondering if they have somehow made a huge mistake and quickly realizing that they haven't.

"Blake let me stop you there," Mr. Andrews, one of the share-holders, says. "It seems that you have the wrong information displayed. Or at least I hope that it is wrong and not an accurate reflection of the return, or lack of it, on our investment in this development."

Mr. Andrews looks embarrassed as he points out the mistake. Blake stops talking and starts to turn, shaking his head, already starting to say there's no mistake. I can see the barely concealed surprise on his face when he learns that Mr. Andrews thinks this is barely a return on his investment. But Blake can't see the terrible figures on display. Not yet.

Blake finally has turned enough to take in the shocking figures on the screen, and for a moment, he stops even trying to speak, his head no longer shaking when he sees the glaringly obvious errors on the screen before him. He looks as embarrassed as Mr. Andrews for a moment, but he shakes it off quickly and gives the shareholders a placating smile, raising his hands in a gesture of calm that I bet he doesn't feel.

"My apologies ladies and gentlemen. It seems that the slide we're currently displaying is the template rather than the actual numbers. Please do ignore those figures and I will have the correct ones sent to you as soon as we're done here," Blake says.

He's covered himself well and he knows the real figures well enough to discuss them as though they are written down in front of him, but the mistake throws him ever so slightly. His confidence has slipped and he's no longer effortlessly charming in his speech and by the end of it, I can tell that some of the shareholders have switched off, bored not just of the information but of the slightly halting delivery of it. No one asks Blake any questions and I get the distinct impression that even the people who were still listening to him by the end of the presentation are still glad that the meeting is almost over.

Once Blake finishes talking and we establish that no one is going to ask him any questions, I try to save the mood by smiling around at the shareholders and telling them the correct figures will be with them by the end of the day. They start to file out of the room, some of them looking annoyed while others just look relieved to get out of the room. As the last one leaves, Blake walks over to the conference room door and shuts it behind them.

"Shit. That was rough," I say. "What do you think happened?"

"I was going to ask you the same question," Blake replies, turning to face me. I am a little bit taken aback by the anger on his face, but I bite my tongue for now and he goes on. "Well? Why don't you tell me what happened?"

"Honestly Blake, I have no idea. I swear when I set up the presentation, that slide had the correct figures on it, and…"

"Enough with the lies," Blake interrupts me. "Why don't you just admit that you wanted me to look bad in front of the shareholders? I couldn't help but notice that there were no issues with any of your slides."

"You seriously think I did this on purpose?" I say, shaking my head in disbelief. "How would sabotaging my own project work Blake? Why on earth would I want to fuck something up that I'm working on myself?"

"Ok, ok," Blake says, holding his hands up and I relax a little bit. "You're not lying. It was a genuine mistake."

I go to open my mouth and tell him that I have no idea at all how this has happened, because it wasn't my mistake. Those are not the figures that were in the presentation when I double and triple checked it. But Blake isn't done talking yet. As he goes on, my little moment of relaxing fades away and I feel myself tensing up more and more as he rants at me. My hands ball into fists at my sides as I sit there in stunned silence for a moment.

"The thing is Kerry, at your level, there's no room for these mistakes, boss's daughter or not. It makes us look incompetent and that's not the look we're going for believe it or not," Blake finishes.

"I realize that," I say, jumping in while I can get a word in. "But like I said, I have no idea what happened."

"I'll tell you what happened," Blake says. "You fucked up. Lately you always mess something up, and quite frankly, it's getting old Kerry."

I am sure he's not done talking, but I as sure as hell am done taking this shit from him. I can feel the blood rushing to my face as humiliation fills me, and I can also feel anger swirling inside of myself. I know those figures were right when I finished up those slides, but I also know I have no way of proving it, and without proof, Blake isn't going to believe me. And somehow, that is even more frustrating than anything.

"Well? What do you have to say for yourself?" Blake snaps.

I don't answer him. I don't think I have the words to do so right now. Instead, I stand up and leave the conference room, ignoring Blake's calls for me to get back here. I can feel tears prickling the backs of my eyes, and Blake can fire me if he wants to for walking away from him like this, but even that is preferable to the idea of him seeing me crying over his words. I will not give him that satisfaction.

KERRY

After I had walked away from Blake earlier in the afternoon, I had gone back to my office, locked the door and had a good cry. I didn't want to cry and I told myself I wasn't crying over Blake and his low opinion of me, I was crying over the fact that something had gone wrong and we had been humiliated in front of the shareholders. I couldn't make myself believe that for even a second and in the end, I stopped trying to rationalize my tears and just let them come. I'm not generally a crier and my reaction felt strange to me, but fighting it only seemed to make it worse, and when I was finally all cried out, I had to admit that I felt better than I had when I had been trying to hold the tears back.

I got myself under control eventually, my hitching breaths returning to normal breaths, and I sorted my makeup out and pulled myself together in time for a meeting I had scheduled with a new potential buyer. I was glad of the meeting. It meant that I had no choice but to pull myself together and get over the scene from earlier. It also meant that there was no chance of me accidentally running into Blake somewhere around the office which was a good thing because I really didn't know what I would say to him if I saw him. It likely wouldn't be nice though. And if I wasn't already fired for walking out on Blake when he clearly wasn't done berating me, I sure would be after I got done giving him a piece of my mind.

I am really glad that today is over now though. Even with my client meeting to distract me from Blake's words, I still felt on edge for the rest of the day. I know what I need. I need to go home, relax, and get my head together ready for tomorrow. I need to be able to think clearly about this, because I know I didn't fuck up those figures, yet they were definitely fucked up by the time we gave the presentation. Is it possible that Blake is trying to make me look bad like he accused me of doing to him? No, I tell myself. That wouldn't make any sense, not when it was him who was made to look stupid in front of the shareholders at the meeting. So who could be doing this then? And why would they want to sabotage us? What could they possibly get out of it?

I have no idea of the answers to any of those questions as I leave my office and head towards the elevator. Hopefully a nice bubble bath and a glass or two of wine will help me to think about it, or better still, will help me forget about it and just relax and worry about this later. That's probably too much to hope for, but I cling to the hope anyway.

The elevator reaches the ground floor and I step out and start making my way across the lobby. I hear someone calling out my name and I almost turn around before I realize that the voice belongs to Blake. Instead of turning around, I hurry up and push open the door and step outside. I am heading for the parking lot and I can still hear Blake calling out behind me. I keep ignoring him. Why can't he take the fucking hint? If I wanted to talk to him, I would have stopped. The only bonus is that out here, Blake isn't my boss and if he starts up with his accusations like he did earlier, I can tell him to go and fuck himself without any repercussions in my job.

Blake is running to catch up with me now and I know there's no way I will reach my car and get in and get away before Blake reaches me so with a sigh, I stop and turn to face him.

"What do you want Blake?" I snap as he jogs towards me.

I ignore the way the sight of him makes my stomach clench in excitement and my clit pulse. Blake reaches me and stops a couple of paces in front of me.

"I want to apologize for earlier," he says.

I don't think he's done talking, but already, I know that I am done listening to him. I hold up a hand, cutting him off before he can waste his breath saying anything else.

"I don't want to hear it Blake," I say. "You made your opinion of me very clear back there and that's really all there is to say on the matter."

I start to turn away again, but Blake catches my arm and stops me. Goosebumps chase each other up and down my arm, radiating out from his touch. Angrily, I snatch my arm away from him.

"I was angry and I lashed out, that's all," Blake says.

"That's all?" I demand, incredulous. "Is this meant to be some sort of a joke? You accused me of sabotaging a big project just to make you look bad. I really can't believe you think I would do that for even a second. No matter how much you might get on my last nerve, I would never do anything to harm the company my father has spent years growing and making a success."

"I know that. That's why I'm trying to apologize. I was wrong, and…" Blake says.

"You know what Blake?" I interrupt him. "I don't care about your half assed apology. As far as I'm concerned, you can go to hell."

I turn and walk away and this time, Blake makes no effort to grab me or call after me. I am feeling strong now and better than I have all day when I get into my car and drive away without looking back at Blake even once. I have no idea how long this feeling will last, but for now, I'll take it.

BLAKE

I am sitting in my office at just past nine the morning after the disastrous meeting and the even more disastrous attempt at apologizing to Kerry. I don't know how I'm going to make her listen to my apology, but I know I have to find a way. I overreacted in the conference room and I know why; I was embarrassed and I took my anger about that out on Kerry. At that point, I was convinced it was her mistake, but even if it was, I know I still shouldn't have gone off at her the way I did. And when she told me she hadn't made the mistake, I should have at least heard her out instead of accusing her of lying about it.

And she was right about what she said to me in the parking lot after work. No matter how much she hates me – and let's be honest, after yesterday's little performance from me, she has every right to hate me – she would never do anything to risk the company that her father helped to build.

So yes. I am going to apologize to Kerry properly, and I am going to do whatever it takes to find a way to make her hear my apology, even if it means I have to take some flak from her. First though, there are some things I need to take care of. I have a few messages from the shareholders with questions now they have the right information to work from. And then I have some people around the office I want to talk to. Because if Kerry didn't make a mistake on the presentation, then something happened to those figures. Just like something happened to the report she showed me before. And maybe even just like something happened to our hotel room booking for the conference too.

If Kerry isn't making these mistakes – and now I've calmed down, I'm inclined to believe that she isn't – then someone is. And considering that it is only Kerry and I who were working on the presentation and the reports, then it has to be someone sabotaging the project intentionally rather than someone just accidentally using the wrong information. No one goes into someone else's files to change their figures unless they have bad intentions. I have no idea who it might be who would do something like that or why they're doing it, but I as sure as hell need to find out and quickly. And when I do, some heads are for sure going to roll.

I stand up and leave my office and head out to my secretary's desk.

"Has anyone been in my office without my knowledge over the last day or two?" I ask her.

She shakes her head.

"No. Of course not," she says.

"Thanks," I comment and keep walking.

I didn't really expect my investigation to be solved that easily and in truth, I didn't expect my secretary to have let anyone wander into my office without my presence or my knowledge, but it seemed like a good idea to ask, just in case something had slipped her mind.

I spend the rest of the working day in between dealing with clients going around the office asking questions of the various staff members that I encounter. I try to keep my questions vague, because I don't expect anyone to confess if someone is trying to sabotage the project and I don't want them to know that I'm starting to catch on and become even more adept at hiding what they're doing.

By the end of the day, I have learned nothing at all. No one seems to be able to answer the questions I am casually asking about the location of certain files, files which if they knew the location meant they also knew the location of the reports for the project Kerry and I are working on. No one seemed uncomfortable or like they were acting strangely when I questioned them and it's starting to feel like all I've done is wasted a good few hours of my own time today.

The only person I haven't talked to is the one person I want to talk to; Kerry. I can't help but wonder if she has any suspicions about who could be doing this. I mean it was me that ended up looking like an asshole in front of the shareholders, but whoever did this must have known that it would look like Kerry was the one to have fucked up the numbers. That makes me think that this isn't so much about me as it is about Kerry, and maybe she knows who is mad at her. I smile to myself at that. Kerry is the sort of woman who most people are mad at most of the time. She's so infuriating that almost anyone could have a grudge against her.

Except that's not true really. The rest of the office seems to get on perfectly fine with Kerry. It's like I am the only person who sees how entitled she can be. So maybe it's not that then. Or maybe it is someone who Kerry has had a falling out with.

I sit down at my desk and start typing out an email to Kerry asking her if she has any idea who might have sabotaged the report. Not only might it give me a lead, but it will also show Kerry that I'm trying my best to fix this. I have almost finished typing out the email when I change my mind and abruptly delete it. Sending this email would be me taking the coward's way out. I have to speak to Kerry properly, face to face.

I get up and head towards Kerry's office. Sasha, her assistant, is at her desk just down the hallway from Kerry's door.

"Is she in?" I ask, nodding towards Kerry's office door.

"No sorry. You just missed her," Sasha replies.

Fuck.

"Ok, thanks," I say, turning away. I pause after a step and turn back. "Has anyone been in Kerry's office unattended over the last few days?"

"No. Not to my knowledge," Sasha replies. "But of course I have my lunch break."

"Thanks," I say, flashing her a smile and then heading back to my own office.

Sasha is right that someone could have sneaked into Kerry's office while she was having her lunch, but I'm starting to think that this is someone tech savvy enough to alter the files remotely and avoid the risk of being seen in either one of our offices.

I put that out of my mind for a moment while I debate what to do about talking to Kerry now she has left for the day. I'm not going to make the mistake of following Kerry out of the building again. Even if Sasha meant that I just missed her literally by a few seconds and I can catch up before she gets in her car and drives off, after the frosty reception I got in the parking lot yesterday, I know that's not the way to get her to hear me out. Instead, I head back to my office. I go inside, sit down, and start to think. I am going to have to catch Kerry tomorrow and apologize then.

I shake my head. I don't want to wait until tomorrow to do this. I want Kerry to know that I'm sorry now and want her to know that I believe that the mistakes weren't hers. And I want her to know that now too. Tonight. Taking a deep breath to calm down my jittering nerves, I pull my cell phone out of my pocket and scroll through my contacts list until I find Kerry's name. I hit call and listen to the ringing sound. I am fully expecting to go through to voicemail and I just have to hope that the message I leave gets Kerry to call me back and sooner rather than later.

"What?" Kerry says, taking my call and surprising me greatly.

In fact, I am so taken aback that she's answered my call at all, that for a moment, I am struck mute.

"Hello?" Kerry says.

"Hi," I manage finally. "Kerry, listen. We need to talk."

"I have nothing to say to you Blake," she says.

"Fine. Then you can just listen to me," I say.

She snorts down her nose but she doesn't end the call and I take that at least to be a good sign.

"I owe you a major apology, I know that. And I want us to be able to work together without it being awkward between us," I say.

"Maybe you should have thought of that before you accused me of sabotaging our project and not being able to do anything right," Kerry puts in.

"Yeah. You're right, I should have," I agree. "And believe me, if I could go back, I wouldn't say those things. But I can't go back can I? So really, all I can do is apologize and that's what I want to do. Tonight. Have dinner with me."

"Are you kidding me?" Kerry snaps.

"No," I say. "I'm deadly serious. Come on Kerry. I'm suggesting a burger or something, not proposing marriage."

Kerry sighs, but when she speaks, I can hear the undertone of amusement in her voice.

"Fine. Pick me up in an hour. And you had better have something better than burgers in mind by the time you get here," she says.

The phone goes dead and I am left holding it to my ear grinning to myself like an idiot. I jump up and head back down the corridor towards Sasha's desk, hoping she's still there. She didn't look like she was getting ready to leave and I think she will be there. I can see her desk now and she is indeed there. I smile to myself. At least one thing has gone right. No actually, two things have gone right, because Kerry agreed to this at all.

KERRY

Blake is due to arrive to pick me up for dinner at any minute. I stand up and glance down at myself in my short black dress wondering if it's a little bit too much or not. Fuck it, I think to myself. Maybe it is too much and maybe it isn't. But I'm not wearing it for Blake, I'm wearing it for me and I like it and that's all that matters. I really hope he took me seriously about going for something a bit better than a burger though. I really will feel stupid sitting in a fast food joint dressed like this.

I hear a car pulling up outside of my house and I glance out of the window. It's Blake's car. I feel a wash of excitement burst over me and I remind myself of two things. Firstly, this is not a date and I shouldn't be this excited about it. And secondly, I am mad at Blake and that's not about to change just because he says he's sorry for yelling at me. I want to see that he means it before I even consider forgiving him.

I slip my feet into my high black heels and grab my purse. I step outside and pause to lock the door behind me, stuffing the key into my purse after I'm done. I walk down towards the car, swaying my hips as I walk. I am wearing the dress for me, but it sure won't hurt to let Blake enjoy it as well. As I make my way towards the car, Blake gets out and moves around to the passenger side door. He opens it and smiles at me, his gaze flitting down to look at my bare, tanned legs.

"You look beautiful," he says.

"Thank you," I say, keeping my voice cool although I am rejoicing inside. "You look nice too."

I'm not just saying it to return the compliment either; he does look nice. He's wearing black jeans and a navy blue t-shirt. The t-shirt is just tight enough to hint at the muscular chest beneath it and I feel my clit tingling as I get into the car. I thank Blake again, this time for holding the car door open for me. He nods and then he slams the car door closed and goes back around to his own side of the car. He gets in and smiles at me.

"Is Mario's alright for dinner your ladyship?" he grins at me as he pulls away from the curb and begins to drive down the road.

"Perfect," I say somewhat grudgingly.

Mario's is my favorite restaurant and knowing we're going there is making being mad at Blake so much harder for me to keep up.

"Who told you?" I ask.

"Sasha," Blake admits, not even trying to pretend that he doesn't know what I mean about who told him that Mario's is my favorite restaurant.

I don't know whether to tell Sasha off tomorrow or give her a bonus. I guess that depends on how tonight goes really I think to myself with a smile.

The drive to the restaurant is pretty short and we pull up outside of the place after a couple of minutes' drive and get out of the car. Blake gives the valet his keys and we step inside and are promptly shown to a table. We sit down and Blake asks for a Diet Coke and I ask for a glass of white wine.

"So," Blake says, when the waiter has moved away. "Before we get started properly, I want to sincerely apologize for yesterday Kerry. I know you would never do anything to risk the company's reputation or business and I know you wouldn't make such an obvious error."

I nod, acknowledging his words, but not forgiving him quite yet. I will though. I can tell by his expression that his apology is genuine. I just don't want him to think he can treat me like shit whenever he wants to and then just come back and say he's sorry and it's all over this easily.

"Really, I am so sorry," Blake says when I don't answer him immediately. He looks at me, clearly waiting for me to say something. "Kerry? Please say something, even if it's just telling me to fuck off."

It takes some effort for me to hide my smile of amusement at his words, but then I think of something and I no longer want to smile. I look down at the table and then I look up, wanting to see Blake's face when I confront him.

"Why did you say any of it then if you didn't mean it?" I ask. "I mean you must have known I wasn't responsible for it even then if you know it now."

"I was angry and I was embarrassed and I know it's no excuse, but I took it out on you and I shouldn't have," Blake says.

His expression is open, his eyes beseeching me to believe him and I find that I do believe him and I just want this apology over and done with now and for us to hopefully move on and be able to work together without it being uncomfortable.

"Fine," I sigh. "Let's just forget about it all ok?"

Blake shakes his head and I frown. I thought this whole thing was meant to be about him getting me to forgive him.

"We can't forget it until you say you forgive me," Blake says with a grin.

I sigh again, loudly this time, and this time it's my turn to shake my head, although I can't stop myself from smiling even as I do it.

"Are you being serious?" I ask.

"Deadly serious," Blake says, nodding his head.

"Fine. I forgive you for being a dick. How's that?" I grin.

"Not quite what I had in mind but I'll take it," Blake laughs.

The waiter returns with our drinks and Blake and I thank him. I watch Blake as he picks his menu up. He raises an eyebrow at me.

"Aren't you hungry?" he asks, nodding down to my untouched menu.

"I'm starving," I smile. "But I know exactly what I'm having. The chicken carbonara followed by the strawberry gelato. It's the best meal in the state."

Blake smiles and puts down his menu.

"Well if it's the best meal in the state, I guess I should have the same then," he says. "It would be silly to miss out."

He flags our waiter down and orders our food and then he turns back to me.

"Like I said, I believe you didn't mess up the figures in that presentation. I didn't either. That means someone is sabotaging our project. Do you have any idea who it could be?" Blake says.

I think for a moment and then I shake my head.

"No," I say. "As far as I know, no one but you and I even had access to the presentation. But even if they did, I can't think who would want to do that to us. Have you pissed anyone off?"

"No," Blake says. "But I don't think it's me they're trying to cause trouble for. I think it's you. I was the one who looked stupid in front of the shareholders, the staff know that you were the one putting the presentation together so they had to know that you would stand a good chance of getting the blame for the figures being wrong. And that report you showed me that was wrong? They knew you would get the blame for that too. And even the room bookings for the conference was something you were dealing with. I know it's not directly linked to the project, but it's another thing that someone has screwed up on purpose to try and make you look incompetent."

"The rooms had nothing to do with this," I say. "That was a genuine accident. Annette took over the booking to save

Sasha some time and she made a mess of it. She admitted it to me and apologized for it."

"Ok, fair enough," Blake says. "But that still leaves us with two instances of work being tampered with to make you look bad."

I nod. He's right; it does. I really don't know who it could be though. I mean why would anyone want to get me in trouble? My team all seem happy enough and I don't really work with anyone on any of the other teams. Maybe it's just jealousy because my father owns half of the company. But surely that's not reason enough to risk losing us a big profit opportunity.

"So who have you pissed off recently?" Blake asks.

"I... no one," I say honestly.

"Oh come on," Blake says, his eyes sparkling in amusement. "Do you really expect me to believe that one?"

"Ok," I laugh. "In fairness, I have no doubt that I've pissed you off several times." I stop laughing and look at Blake with a serious expression. "But really. I don't know of anyone who would do this. And I can't even begin to imagine why they're trying to make me look bad."

"Ok. I'll keep digging," Blake says.

"What do you mean keep digging?" I ask. "You mean you've already been looking into this?"

Blake nods his head.

"Yeah. I've asked around a bit today – nothing that would sound like I suspected anything, just general enquiries you know – but as of yet, I haven't heard anything useful.

Someone will slip up though. People who do this kind of shit and get away with it a few times always end up getting cocky and giving themselves away somehow."

"By then I could have been sacked and we could have lost half of our business and some of our shareholders," I say.

"The shareholders aren't going anywhere. They're making money and that's their only real concern. We won't lose business because of it – your clients have all been with you for years and if anything odd comes up, they'll believe you when you tell them it wasn't you behind it. As for getting sacked though, that's a definite possibility if you keep refusing to talk to me in public," Blake says.

"Ok, let's make a deal," I smile. "I won't refuse to talk to you in public if you don't yell at me, disbelieve me, and generally make a fool out of me without even hearing me out."

"Ouch," Blake winces. "You're making me sound like the boss from hell."

"You said it," I shrug.

"But you were thinking it right?" Blake says.

He looks a little bit hurt and I can't help but feel badly about this. I did say I was willing to forgive and forget it after all. I relent and I shake my head.

"Not quite the boss from hell. Just the boss that doesn't listen when he should. Now do we have a deal or not?" I say.

"Yes, we do. As long as we can promise not to mention this again for the rest of the night," he says.

"Deal," I grin, extending my hand over the table.

Blake shakes my hand and shivers run up my arm, reminding me that the chemistry between Blake and I has most definitely not gone anywhere. The waiter appears with our meals then and we have to unlink our hands. I am a little bit disappointed – I was enjoying the feeling of Blake's palm pressed against mine. I try to shake the thought away. I came here to hear Blake out, not for anything else.

I know even as I think it that I am lying to myself. I mean I did want to hear Blake out, but I also wanted something more. As much as I tell myself I don't like Blake, I know that's no longer true. I do like him. I like him far too much. And the dinner, the dress, the skyscraper heels – to me, they're all about one thing. Getting Blake in my bed and having a repeat of our night in the hotel. Only this time, without the fight afterwards.

Blake smiles up at me after the waiter has left and he has tried his first bite of the carbonara.

"You were right," he grins. "This is amazing."

"I could eat it every day and never get sick of it," I say.

"Right. So I now officially know your favorite food, which I think is the first non-work thing I've ever learned about you," Blake says.

"And it's still more than I know about you," I point out.

"Oh. I have a refined palate. My favorite food is pizza," Blake says.

"Oh no way," I laugh. "I mean pizza is nice enough, but it's not favorite food material."

"It's bread, cheese and pepperoni. What part of that is not to love?" Blake says, raising an eyebrow.

"Well I guess when you put it like that, nothing," I say.

Blake grins and goes back to his meal.

"This is a pretty close second though," he says.

I smile and eat in silence for a moment. I want to get to know Blake, but I don't know where to start without feeling like I am quizzing him. Blake saves me from having to question him by smiling up at me.

"At the risk of sounding like a massive dick, I have to say that nothing beats a real Italian pizza," he says.

"As in you've been to Italy?" I ask.

Blake nods his head.

"Yes. And you don't realize until you go there how bad our versions of Italian food are. I mean they taste nice and every-thing, but they're a long way from being authentic," he says.

"Oh I can imagine," I say. "Whereabouts in Italy did you go?"

"Milan," Blake replies. "And then Naples. I did a fair bit of traveling when I was younger. What about you?"

"I've been to Mexico a few times and I've been to Rio and that's it," I say.

"I reckon I'd like Rio," Blake says.

"Oh you would," I say. "It's a beautiful city and the people are so friendly."

Blake smiles at me and then he notices my empty wine glass. He nods towards it.

"Would you like another glass of wine?" he asks.

"Are you trying to get me drunk?" I ask with a raised eyebrow.

"That depends," Blake grins. "Do I need to?"

"I'd have to say yes to that," I reply. "But only because I really want another glass of wine."

Blake laughs and signals to our waiter and orders me another glass of wine. While we wait for it, we finish up our meals and our waiter brings our desserts with my wine. We thank him and he nods and moves away from us. I take a big sip of wine and hold my glass aloft.

"To actually being civil to each other," I say.

"I'll drink to that," Blake laughs, clinking his Diet Coke glass against my wine glass. "I'm rather liking this truce."

"Me too," I admit after drinking another mouthful of wine.

I put the glass down and pick my spoon up. I spoon up a small bit of gelato and I slowly lick it from the spoon, looking Blake in the eye the whole time I do it. I can see him squirming in his seat and I look down at the table, covering my mouth with my hand for a moment while I grin to myself. I know the effect I'm having on him. It is the exact effect I was hoping for. I eat a bit more of the gelato without looking up.

I finally risk a glance up through my eye lashes. Blake is eating his own gelato, but his eyes are still trained firmly on me and I feel a shiver of anticipation run down my spine as I run my tongue over my lips. I bring my head back up and eat another spoonful of the gelato, looking Blake in the eye the whole time. I can feel my heart beating a little bit too fast and my pussy clenches when Blake moans under his breath. I smile and then I start eating the gelato in a normal fashion. Blake moans again and then he smiles at me and shakes his head.

"That was quite a show," he comments quietly.

"You should see what I do for an encore," I wink.

"I can't wait," Blake fires back.

"Oh but you'll have to," I say with a smile. I glance around and then lean in closer to Blake. "It's not the sort of party trick I can do in front of other people."

"Even better," Blake smiles.

I lean back in my seat and sip my wine. I am being a lot more forward than I normally would be, but I don't care. I want Blake and I no longer care if he knows it. He's making no secret of the fact that he wants me too and to be honest, now we've both let our guards down a bit, I am actually enjoying his company and I think, or at least I hope, that he would say the same thing about me.

I am feeling brave and I slowly slip one of my feet out of its shoe. I run my bare toes over Blake's calf, moving them up his leg towards his knee. I run them across his inner thigh and I hesitate for a moment and then I decide if I'm going to do it, then I might as well do it like I mean it. I move my foot to his cock and begin to move my toes lightly over it through his jeans. Blake squirms slightly in his chair and looks at me. He swallows hard as I move my foot a little bit faster. I pick my glass up and drain the last of my wine as I keep working Blake. I can feel how hard he is already.

"Would you like another drink?" he asks, his voice husky.

"Yes," I smile. "But I thought maybe we could have this one at my place."

Blake smiles, but he gives me no indication of whether or not he thinks that's a good idea. He looks away from me and signals for our waiter and I figure I have pushed my luck with this too far too quickly. It looks like Blake wants us to have the drink here.

"Can we have the check please," Blake says to the waiter when he reaches our table.

I bite my lip to stop myself from cheering out loud. He has taken my hint after all, and I know what's going to happen after our drink. I know only too well and I can hardly wait. I pull my toes away from Blake as the waiter nods and moves back away from the table. I figure Blake will want to get himself back under control before we have to walk across the restaurant floor in front of the other diners. I push my foot back into my shoe and Blake smiles at me.

"You know, two of us can play at that game Kerry," he says.

"Huh?" I say, not quite sure what he means.

He leans towards me, shuffling to the edge of his seat and he plays with his napkin with one hand. His other hand skims my knee and then runs over my inner thigh, spreading tingles through my skin and making me instantly wet. I bite down on my bottom lip to stop myself from moaning as his fingers run over the top of my panties, teasing my clit beneath them. I gasp in a breath as Blake pushes my panties to one side and begins to rub my clit hard and fast. I sit back in my seat, my back against the chair back, pushing my ass to the edge of the seat itself. I grip the table's edge with both hands, trying to look casual, like I'm just sitting comfortably. I don't know if I am pulling the look off or not, and right now, I have pretty much stopped caring. All I can focus on is the feel of Blake's expert fingers working my clit, bringing me closer and closer to my climax.

The waiter reappears beside our table and still Blake doesn't stop working me. I force myself to smile at the waiter like everything is normal and I'm not about to come on the spot. He places the check on the table.

"Was everything to your liking?" he asks us.

I smile and nod.

"Yes, thank you," I say, pleased that my voice, while not exactly normal, isn't quite as breathy as I feared it might be.

"Everything was perfect," Blake says with a polite smile at the waiter. "Thank you."

The waiter nods and moves away from us once more and I let out the breath that I have been holding as Blake still works my clit. I take a breath, about to tell him to stop, but then he hits the sweet spot and I can't bring myself to ask him to stop. I never want him to stop. I want him to keep working me like this all night long, pushing me closer and closer to my climax.

I grip the edge of the table more tightly with one hand, and with the other, I pick my napkin up, bringing it to my mouth like I am wiping my lips. In truth, I am biting down on the napkin as my orgasm blasts through my body, trying to stop myself from screaming out loud. I manage to hold in my screams, but I can't stop the shudder of pleasure that runs through my body as my orgasm spreads out through me.

Blake smiles at me as he pulls his fingers away from me. He puts his hand back on the table. I can see my juices glistening on his fingers and he seems to notice at the same time as I do. He raises his hand to his mouth and sucks on his index finger.

"Mmmm," he moans as he moves onto the next finger.

I shuffle in my seat, my clit still pulsing from the orgasm that I am barely starting to come down from, and now from desire too as I watch Blake lick my juices off his fingers. God he's so fucking hot and he knows exactly how to work me into a state of utter frenzy.

He stops sucking his fingers and picks up the check and I take advantage of the moment where his attention isn't focused on me and pull my panties straight. I gasp slightly as the fabric brushes over my swollen and tender clit and I smile to myself as I imagine what it's going to be like when we get to my place and Blake touches me again, and this time, I will be able to make as much noise as I like.

Blake puts some money down with the check and I reach for my purse. Blake frowns and I smile.

"What? I'm just paying for my half," I say.

Blake shakes his head.

"It's on me," he says.

"Fine," I agree. "But the next time is my treat."

"There's going to be a next time?" Blake asks with that eyebrow raised once more and his mouth twisting into a grin at the outer corners.

I love the raised corner smile on him. It's so sexy and it makes me want to grab him and ride him right here at the table.

"Oh I think there might be," I say, running my tongue over my lips after I speak.

Blake nods after a moment.

"Yes. I think you might be right there," he agrees. "Are you ready to go?"

"More than ready," I tell him.

I'm not sure if he means am I ready to go from the restaurant or am I ready to go in the bedroom, but it doesn't matter, because either way, what I said covers us as it's the answer to both questions. I stand up as Blake does and he offers me his arm which I take. As we head across the restaurant, I am conscious of the fact that my pussy is slippery with moisture and I wonder if Blake is still hard and if he is, are the other diners noticing it. No one gives us more than a brief glance as we pass and I think that we're most likely in the clear. I start to giggle slightly and Blake looks at me with an amused look on his face.

"What's so funny?" he asks me.

I shake my head.

"Nothing. Just something I was thinking about," I say.

"Oh come on. Share," Blake grins.

I lean closer to him so I can whisper into his ear.

"I was just thinking that it's funny that I've just come in my panties in the middle of this place and no one around us was observant enough to notice," I say. "And I don't think any of them have noticed that you're hard either."

I can see he is hard by a quick glance down, but to be fair, if I was sitting at a table and someone passed me like this, I probably wouldn't notice either. I just want Blake to know that I know he's as turned on by all of this as I am.

When I finish whispering to him, I quickly flick my tongue over his ear lobe, and then I pull back from him.

"I don't care who knows how much I want you," Blake says.

I playfully slap his arm and shush him, even though he barely spoke above a whisper anyway. He grins at me and then he looks up to thank the host as we reach the front of the restaurant.

"Thank you, sir, ma'am. Enjoy the rest of your evening," he says in reply to our thanks.

"Oh we will," Blake and I both say together.

The host gives us a knowing smile and we keep walking until we're outside of the place and then I start to laugh again.

"He *so* knew what we were getting upto in there," I say.

"Like I said, I don't care who knows how much I want you," Blake says with a shrug.

I feel a warmth inside of me and I have to really fight myself to resist the urge to pull Blake's face down to mine and kiss him. I am glad I resisted the urge because at that moment, the valet pulls up beside us in Blake's car. He gets out, leaving the engine running as Blake walks me around to the passenger side and opens the door for me. I get into the car and thank Blake and he closes the door. I take the couple of seconds while Blake thanks the valet and tips him to compose myself a little bit, and by the time Blake gets into the car, I am pretty much in control of myself enough that I don't pounce on him instantly. Blake pulls away from the curb and begins to head towards my place.

"So where are you planning on taking me for your treat then?" he asks with a soft laugh.

"Well seeing as you suggested a burger for this evening before I put you right on that one, I don't know. Maybe McDonalds," I laugh.

"See you think that would be an insult. I think it would be a perfectly acceptable meal," Blake laughs with me.

I shake my head as I laugh.

"You're so different to how I thought you would be," I admit.

"As are you," Blake admits. "I guess we both judged each other too quickly."

"Yeah. And then we were both too stubborn to make any effort to see if maybe we had been wrong about each other," I agree.

"Are you saying what I think you're saying?" Blake asks me.

"That depends on what you think I'm saying," I tell him.

My heart is pounding suddenly and I am nervous for what Blake is thinking.

"That we're both dicks," Blake laughs.

I feel myself relax and I laugh with him, nodding my head.

"Yeah, I reckon that about sums it up," I say.

The car stops moving then and I realize we're at my place already. I get out without waiting for Blake to come and open my door. Blake gets out too and he follows me up my path to my front door. We go inside and Blake closes the front door behind him, following me into the lounge. I turn to face him and smile.

"What would you like to drink? I have vodka, scotch, wine or beer," I say.

"Oh, you're still doing that?" Blake says, looking a little bit disappointed.

"Doing what?" I ask, my confusion written all over my face I'm sure.

Blake's disappointment fades as he grins instead.

"Pretending that me coming here was really about us having a drink together," he says.

He closes the gap between us and pulls me into his arms. I go into them willingly enough and when Blake kisses me, I make no pretence at resisting him. Instead, I melt into him and move my lips against his with a ferocity that scares me a little bit.

I am hungry for Blake. I want him more than I have ever wanted anyone or anything, and if his kiss is anything to go by, I am in for a night I will never forget. Blake pushes one hand into my hair, mashing my lips even more tightly against his. His other hand is on my waist, pressing my body against his. My own hands move all over Blake's back beneath his t-shirt, feeling the taut muscles there.

I pull back from the kiss, although I don't want it to end. I smile at Blake's confused look as I wriggle out of his arms and take his hand in mine. I start to walk, pulling him with me, and he smiles again as I reach the stairs and start to climb them and he works out why I have stopped kissing him for the moment.

BLAKE

I follow Kerry, my hand tingling in hers as she leads me up her stairs to her bedroom. She is confident, magnificent and I can't wait to show her how much I want her.

I had no idea tonight would end like this when I invited Kerry out for dinner. Of course it's the exact ending I would have chosen if I had been given a choice in the matter, but I really didn't think it would happen. I would have been happy just to have Kerry forgive me for being such an asshole to her after the shareholder meeting. Instead, I get both forgiveness and this amazing session that we're about to have, and I am a whirling mess of lust and longing, my cock hard and aching in my jeans.

We're in Kerry's bedroom now and she turns to me and I wrap her in my arms, pulling her closer to me, my lips brushing hers as my hands roam over her back. She pulls at my T shirt, and for a second, our lips leave each other while she pulls it over my head. I can feel her hands on my bare back now and I feel my skin tingling where she touches me, leaving me wanting more of her. I think I'll always want more of her, no matter how much of her I get.

I reach around to the back of her dress and pull the zipper down, my tongue exploring Kerry's mouth as I go. I pull the dress down over her hips and then I release it and let it fall to the floor.

I walk Kerry towards the bed in the center of the room. She reaches down and opens my jeans as we move. She gets them open as we reach the bed. She's not wearing a bra and I can feel her hard nipples against my chest, and I want to touch them, to suck on them, to make them even harder.

I push Kerry backwards and she tumbles onto the bed. I take a second to remove the rest of my clothes as Kerry kicks off her shoes and discards her panties on the ground. When we're both naked, I clamber onto the bed, hovering over Kerry with my mouth above her breasts. I lean down and suck one into my mouth. As I suck it, I work the nipple of her other breast in my fingers.

Within seconds, Kerry is writhing beneath me as I work her nipples, sending shockwaves of pleasure through her body. She puts her head back, moaning as I keep working her and I move my free hand down her body and find her clit, working both of her nipples and her clit in time with each other. The sensation pushes Kerry over the edge and she moans loudly as liquid gushes from her pussy and her muscles tense up making her body feel tight and rigid.

I release her nipple from my mouth, watching as her damp skin puckers as the night air caresses it. I kiss up her chest and up her neck, finding her lips with mine and kissing her hard on the mouth. I still work her clit, loving the way she tenses up beneath me, moaning into my mouth as I rub my fingers over her most sensitive part. I kiss down her neck again as she clings to me, panting into my ear and sending fire racing through me. I love knowing the effect I can have on her body is as intense as the effect that she can have on mine.

Another orgasm rips through her and she makes a strangled sound that's almost a whimper, still clinging to me, her legs wrapped around me squeezing me tighter as her pleasure moves through her. I move my fingers from her clit and kiss her and she clenches herself against me. She takes a moment to collect herself and then she pushes me onto my back. I let her move me, and she rolls with me, coming up and straddling me across my thighs.

She smiles down at me and then she reaches out and takes my cock in her fist. I feel heat flood out from my cock and through my body as Kerry begins to work her magic on me, her grip firm and confident as she strokes me. I swallow hard, closing my eyes and letting the pleasure caress me. I lay that way for a moment and then I open my eyes, watching Kerry's gorgeous body in the moonlight that streams in through the still open curtains at the window, making her look luminescent and silvery.

I allow myself to become lost in the moment and float on a wave of euphoria, but then I bite down on my lip and rein myself back in, not wanting to come before I am inside of Kerry once more.

Kerry is attuned to my body and she senses I am close to the edge and takes her hand away from my cock. She runs both hands over my chest and stomach, spreading goosebumps over my skin. She leans forward and kisses me hard on the mouth. I wrap my arms around her, pulling her down on top of me. I can feel the heat from her pussy on my cock and I know I have to have her right now. I reach down and grab my cock, lining it up with her pussy. She pulls her lips from mine and sits up and then she lifts herself and lowers herself down onto my cock impaling herself on my length. She gasps as I fill her all the way up and I gasp with her, feeling her hot, tight flesh around me. I slide inside of her easily and she begins to move up and down on me.

I watch as her breasts jiggle as she moves. She looks amazing, like a Goddess or an Amazonian warrior as she moves. and the feelings that spread through me are almost impossible to bite back. I know it won't be long until I can't hold my climax at bay any longer and I reach up and catch hold of Kerry.

As I grab her, I buck my hips and throw her to the side. I roll with her, not breaking our contact, staying deep inside of her, and I come to land on top of her. She grins up at me, her eyes heavy with lust. I lean down and kiss her as I thrust into her, upping my pace until she's moaning into my mouth, her body writhing beneath me as her pussy clenches around my cock, spreading waves of fire through me.

I kiss her neck, breathing in the scent of her, kissing and licking her skin. I know I can't hold back any longer, and I let go, plunging all of the way into Kerry and letting my climax overtake me.

Pleasure coasts through my body, making me tingle all over. I gasp in a breath and hold it as I let my orgasm wash over me, carrying me away to a place where I am nothing but a ball of nerve endings.

Finally, my orgasm starts to fade, and although it's good to fill my burning lungs again, I already miss the feeling of coming inside of Kerry. I kiss her hard on the mouth and then I roll off her and we lay side by side panting for air. When I feel like I'm back to myself a little bit, I turn my head and look at Kerry with a grin.

"Remind me why we waited so long to do that," I say.

"Because we're idiots clearly," Kerry laughs.

She rolls towards me and I wrap her in my arms, holding her tightly against me as I feel my eyes starting to close. Even in my wildest dreams, I didn't think tonight would turn out like this, but I'm so glad it did, because truly, there's nowhere on earth I would rather be right now than right here with Kerry falling asleep in my arms.

KERRY

I can't believe almost a month has passed since the night I took Blake back to my place after we went out for dinner so that he could apologize to me about the way he carried on when there was an issue in our presentation.

The morning after that night, I woke up to find Blake already awake and watching me sleep. I opened my mouth to tell him once more that us sleeping together had been a mistake, but the truth was, it didn't feel like a mistake, and instead, I just wished him a good morning, a sentiment he returned. We ended up being late for work that morning because it seemed we wanted each other to have a very good morning.

That night, I fulfilled my promise and took Blake out for burgers and fries, and we really haven't looked back since that day. It's strange in some ways that I've gone from dreading seeing Blake to looking forward to seeing him and I've gone from that feeling of annoyance when I see him to a feeling of butterflies in my tummy when I see him.

It's worked out well though, and not just because we can't seem to keep our hands off each other now and I am in an almost constant state of arousal. It's worked out well for us working together too. Now that we're not constantly at each other's throats, our work is getting done much faster and much better and our joint project is going really well. In fact, it's on track to be one of the most successful projects the company has ever taken on.

"Kerry? Are you alright?" a voice says.

It's my dad and his voice pulls me out of my head and I force my attention away from watching Blake across the room and focus instead on my dad. I smile at him.

"Yeah I'm fine. Why?" I say.

"I don't know. You seem distracted," he says.

"I was just thinking about something," I say. "If we change the layout of the new estate ever so slightly, we can..."

"Stop," my dad says, raising his palm.

I frown at him.

"What? You don't think it'll work?" I ask, surprised at this because I've been over it enough times to know it's at least possible and I'm shocked my dad doesn't think it's at least worth looking at.

"I'm sure it will if you've been giving it your attention," my dad says, his face breaking into a smile as he gestures around himself. "But in case you haven't noticed, this is a party Kerry. You're meant to be enjoying yourself and not thinking about work."

I can't help but return his smile. I should have known what he was implying. He looks at me questioningly.

"So do you think you can manage one night where you have a good time and don't think about work?" he asks.

I smile wider and nod.

"I think I can just about manage that," I say, although I'm not actually sure that's true.

I'm not stressing out about work – that would be bad, I can accept that. I am thinking about it because I am excited about the project and for that reason, I don't want to not think about it. But I've told my dad I can have one night where I focus on something else, so I'll at least try not to think about work. For maybe the next half an hour or so. Just to see how it goes.

"See. You're smiling already," my dad says. He follows my gaze and gives me a knowing smile. "Ah, and there was me thinking I'd cheered you up. I should have known better."

I want to deny the fact that it's Blake that's making me smile, that it's Blake that I can't keep my eyes away from, but what would be the point? My dad knows me well enough to know better than that, and besides, he's spent years trying to push Blake and I closer together. It's not like he can complain when it's finally worked, even if we did end up even closer than he originally thought we might.

"So are you two together now?" my dad asks me.

I sigh and shake my head.

"No. I mean I don't know really. Like we haven't made anything official but we're dating I guess you could say," I reply.

I get on well with my dad and I can talk to him about pretty much anything, but I draw the line at telling him that Blake and I are fucking like rabbits pretty much daily.

"As long as you're happy, that's all that matters," my dad says. "And I think it's fair to say you look happy."

I nod. I am happy. Really happy. Even more so now I notice Blake cutting across the room and heading towards us. My dad gives me another one of those knowing smiles.

"Well as much as I'd like to stand and talk to you all night Kerry, I have people I need to go and chat to," he grins.

"Ok," I say. And then quieter, "thanks dad."

He winks at me and disappears into the crowd of milling guests just as Blake reaches me.

"Something I said?" he asks, nodding towards my dad's hastily retreating back.

I laugh and shake my head.

"No. Something I said. That's my dad's subtle way of giving us some space," I say.

"Oh I see," Blake says. He grins and holds his hand out to me. "Well we don't want to let his sacrifice be in vain, do we. Let's dance."

I take Blake's hand and let him lead me into the center of the floor where other people are also dancing. Within a single moment, I am in Blake's arms and my body is responding to him, shivers of desire going through me everywhere we touch. I am tempted to tilt my head up and rub my lips across Blake's lips, but I resist the urge. We haven't talked about what we are, if we're anything, and until we do, I don't want to give anyone at the office anything concrete to talk about with us. It's bad enough being the daughter of one of the bosses without getting talked about for kissing the other one as well.

I'll live with the gossip and the snide remarks when people think I'm out of ear shot if Blake and I stand a chance of going the distance because he's worth it and what we could have together might just be worth it. But I draw the line at being a talking point in the office if we're just having casual sex with each other and Blake doesn't see any potential future for us.

Instead of kissing Blake, I close my eyes and rest my head on his chest, letting him guide me around the floor. It feels like we're gliding on air, like we are the only two people in the room at that moment, and I just relax, let go of all of my thoughts and let myself enjoy it. I love the feel of Blake's strong, warm arms wrapped around me, and I love the scent of him filling my nose.

I don't want to leave Blake's arms, but the song ends and I know it will look bizarre if I don't and so reluctantly, I pull back and smile up at him. He returns my smile.

"Should we grab a drink?" I say and Blake nods.

We make our way off the dance floor, grabbing glasses of champagne from a passing waiter and moving out onto the terrace where we can chat a little bit without having to yell at each other to be heard over the music.

"You look nice tonight," Blake says, looking me up and down and taking in my midnight blue body con dress.

"You don't have to sound so surprised," I smile.

Blake laughs and shakes his head.

"You need to learn how to take a compliment," he says.

"Ok and how does that work then?" I say, playing along with him.

"Well, you say thank you, so do you. Do you want to try it?" Blake says.

"But what if I don't want to say you look nice?" I say.

"Then I'll be deeply wounded," Blake says, clutching his chest.

I laugh and dig him with my elbow.

"Ok. I think I'm ready to try it again," I say.

"You look nice tonight," Blake says.

"Thank you. You look ok too I guess," I grin.

"Well you're getting there, but we're going to have to work on it a little bit more I think," Blake says.

I move closer to Blake and stretch up on my tip toes and lean in closer to him so that I can whisper in his ear.

"How about you look so hot I want to lick you all over?" I whisper.

Blake moans and I smirk.

"I take it that was the right answer," I say, still whispering in his ear.

I hear a cough behind me and I move back from Blake quickly. He turns away slightly as I glance over my shoulder to see who is approaching us. I relax when I see it's only Lisa. She knows about Blake and I and our thing that might not even be a thing.

"Am I interrupting something?" she asks.

I am dying to say yes. I know if I do, she'll go back inside with no hard feelings, but before I can answer, Blake shakes his head.

"No, of course not," he says, unaware of just how much Lisa knows.

"Good," Lisa says. "I just need a bit of air."

"You do look a bit peaky," I say to Lisa, frowning.

Now she's said that, I realize she doesn't look well at all.

"I'm ok really. I'm just a bit too hot," Lisa says waving away my concern.

I glance at Blake and he shrugs.

"Let me go and grab you a glass of water," he says.

He goes back inside before Lisa can reply and I turn to where she's taken a seat on the patio.

"Come on Lisa. There's just us here now. Are you really alright?" I ask, moving to sit beside her.

She nods her head.

"I'm fine Kerry. Honestly I am. I've just got some killer

cramps that's all. I've been overdoing it work wise and it always interferes with my cycle when I do that. I've finally started my period this afternoon, but it's well over two weeks late and I'm suffering with it a bit," she says.

"Oh right," I say. "God Lisa, you shouldn't be working hard enough to affect your health like that."

She waves away my concern once more. I sigh and shake my head.

"So were you worried when you were late?" I ask.

"No," Lisa replies. "It's happened before so I had a fair idea what it was. Besides, it's not like I thought I could be pregnant. We're not all getting it every five minutes like you are."

I feel heat flooding my cheeks as I laugh. I wish it was every five minutes. Even now I am craving Blake's touch. At the thought of him touching me, my pussy clenches slightly.

"It's more like every ten minutes," I say.

Lisa and I burst out laughing and we're still laughing when Blake comes back with a glass of iced water for Lisa. He sits down with us and holds the glass out to Lisa. She thanks him and takes the glass and sips the water despite not needing it really.

"What's so funny?" Blake asks, looking from Lisa to me.

"Just that apparently my perception of time is slightly off," Lisa says.

Blake looks at her in total confusion and that sets us both off laughing again. Blake gives up trying to work out what we're laughing at. Instead, he stands back up again.

"I'm going to let you two catch up. There's a client in there I wanted to grab and have a quick chat with anyway," he says.

I nod and watch Blake head back for the house.

"Sorry," Lisa says. "I think I scared him away. And that was without me even mentioning my cycle around him at all."

That gets us laughing once more, but somewhere in our laughter I realize something. Lisa isn't the only one who's period is late. I am about five or six days overdue myself. Could I be...? No, I tell myself. Of course I'm not. I'm just like Lisa – over working a bit that's all. And the fact that I have never been late because of work stresses ever before is completely irrelevant.

~

I woke up early the Monday after the party. I remember that I jumped up out of bed quickly and hurried to the bathroom. I had checked my panties and sighed when I saw that they were clean. I had been hoping for blood and I had convinced myself that that day would be the day I saw it. After the party on Saturday, finally starting my period was all I had thought about. Well except for during the first couple of hours directly after the party of course.

For those few hours, all I had thought about was Blake. He had come home with me and although he had successfully taken my mind off my period for the time we were together, once it was over and he had fallen asleep, I had lain awake wondering if I could be pregnant and cursing Lisa for putting this idea in my mind. I never should have asked her what was wrong at the party and I wouldn't have even started thinking about my own period being late.

Sunday morning had dragged by and Blake had sensed something was wrong with me. In the end, I realized it couldn't go on like this, that the not knowing was making me act strangely, and I had told myself that I would give it until this morning, and if there was still no sign of my period, I would do a pregnancy test, and then when it comes back negative, I can relax. Because it has to be negative doesn't it. I mean it's not like we haven't been careful – I have been on birth control pills the whole time me and Blake have been sleeping together, and I am almost certain that I haven't missed any.

I've been to the pharmacy and bought a test. I wonder what the checkout girl thought about me buying the test before eight am. Did she think I was panicked or excited? Did she even notice what I was buying or care about it? Probably not to be honest. Anyway, do I even care what she thought about it? The truth is, I don't much care what she thought about my purchase; it's just easier to focus on that than it is to focus on my real problem.

Now I have the test home and I've peed on the stick and it's the moment of truth. Suddenly I am nervous. I mean you hear of people getting pregnant on birth control pills all the time don't you? And I can't help but wonder what it means if I'm not pregnant. Like why would my cycle have just stopped? Would it be easy to fix, whatever caused it? Would it just be something simple like overworking like Lisa, or something more sinister like... no, I won't go there. I won't start thinking about the C word.

I am starting to hyperventilate and I tell myself to calm down and just see what the test has to say before I worry about anything else. I glance at my watch. Less than ten seconds to go. I keep staring at the second hand on my watch, half of me willing it to slow down and half of me willing it to move faster. Of course it does neither, but the time soon passes.

I reach out for the test and take a deep breath. I close my eyes for a moment then I open them and breathe out. I pick the test up and look at the window.

I am pregnant.

BLAKE

I look up from my screen and smile when Kerry steps into my office. My smile widens when she closes the door behind herself and leans on it for a moment. She smiles back at me, but it's not her lust filled smile and I think she probably hasn't shut the door so we can make love. It's a tentative smile, like she's worried about something. My own smile slips as I peer at her. I hate to see her looking so unsure of herself like this.

"What's wrong?" I ask, standing up and coming around to her side of my desk.

She just shakes her head and for a moment, I think I've gotten it wrong and there's nothing going on with her. But then I see the tears forming in her eyes. She looks down at the ground trying to hide them, but she's too late. I cover the gap between us and take her hands in mine, frowning with concern. Kerry isn't one of those women who cry at anything. Something really bad must have happened to get this reaction from her. I swear if someone has hurt her, I'll kill them, and I do mean that literally.

"Talk to me Kerry," I say. "Tell me what's wrong. Please."

She shakes her head again, but this time she looks up at me which is an improvement on a couple of seconds earlier. She sighs loudly, a sound full of despair. It hurts me to hear her so upset and not be able to do anything about it.

"Firstly, I need you to know I didn't do this on purpose. I did everything right, or at least I thought I did. And if you don't want to stay, then I get it and there will be no hard feelings," she says.

My first thought is the new development project Kerry and I are working on together. She must have made some kind of mistake on it, but that doesn't make sense of the last part of her sentence. I would hardly just walk away from the project because there was a mistake no matter what it was or who had made it. Plus, it's not like Kerry would come in here on the verge of crying because of a mistake on a project. She's no drama queen. Whatever this is, it has to be something bigger than that. Is she ill and worried that she's forcing me to stick around? That she'll somehow be a burden on me or whatever? I don't want her to be ill obviously, but even if she is, I won't be going anywhere and she could never ever be a burden to me.

The silence between us is stretching out now and it's killing me. With each second that passes, I am imagining worse and worse scenarios. I realize Kerry likely isn't going to go any further without a little bit more prompting though and I'm happy to oblige with that. Anything to get her talking and find out what's going on here.

"Kerry, please, just tell me what's going on," I say. "Whatever it is, I promise I won't be angry, and trust me, it can't possibly be worse than what I'm imagining."

She must hear the desperation in my voice, because she nods her head, takes a deep breath and tells me what is happening.

"I'm pregnant," she says.

Did I hear that right? No I can't have. I thought Kerry said… she did say it. I know she did. I had all of that worry pressing down on me for nothing.

"You mean we're having a baby?" I say, needing her to confirm I didn't hear wrong or misunderstand somehow before I let myself react to the news.

Kerry nods her head.

"Yes. But like I said, I understand if you want to walk away from this, from me. I mean we hardly planned for this did we?" she says.

"Well no, we didn't, but I couldn't be happier Kerry honestly," I say. "Just because we didn't plan this doesn't mean it's not the best news I've had in ages."

"Really?" she says, frowning at me, willing it to be true. "Because if you need some time, I get it, and I would rather you just tell me now if you're not sure about this."

I smile at her, a smile so wide and full of such happiness that it makes my cheeks ache.

"Really Kerry. I'm sure. More sure than I have ever been of anything," I say, laughing and pulling her into my arms. "I can't believe you thought I would want to walk away from you and our child."

"It wasn't so much that I thought you would want to, it was just if you did want to, I didn't want you to feel like you had to stick around," Kerry says. "If you're in our lives, I want to know it's because you want to be, not because you feel like you have to be."

She finishes talking and then she pulls back slightly from my embrace and looks up at me and smiles. I return her smile and then I lean down and kiss her. What starts as a gentle, tender kiss soon becomes a hungry kiss, full of passion. Hearing that Kerry is going to be having my baby only makes me want her more. I never want to let her out of my sight and I don't want to let her out of my arms either.

She presses herself against me, her kiss as passionate and ferocious as my own. My heart is racing and my cock is rock hard and I know she can feel it pressing against her. I have to have her right now before I explode.

It takes every bit of will power I have to extract myself from Kerry's arms, but I do it. I move away from her for long enough to lock the office door and then we come back together again, our mouths finding each other, our hands roaming all over each other's bodies. I pull my mouth from Kerry's mouth, kissing down her neck as I stretch my arms out behind her and swipe my desk clean at one side. Pens and pencils and paperwork fall to the ground, a mixed up mess. Normally, a mess like this would make me anxious, but right now, I barely even notice it. That's what Kerry does to me. She consumes me so completely that she becomes the center of my world, the only thing that matters to me and the only thing I register in the moment.

I reach down and push Kerry's skirt up over her hips and onto her waist, and then I cup her ass cheeks and lift her, sitting her on the edge of the desk in the newly cleared space. She wraps her arms around my shoulders and moves her face closer to mine. I kiss her, but it's a brief kiss, the kind I know will leave her wanting more. And more is exactly what she's going to get.

I reach up and behind me and gently remove Kerry's arms from around me, and then I fall to my knees in front of her and grip her inner thighs, pushing her legs wide apart. I move into the gap I have made, so close to her now that I can smell the lust coming off her pussy in waves. I push her damp panties to one side, moaning when I see how wet she is beneath them. I lean in and press my tongue into her slit, licking her as I move my tongue towards her clit.

I find her clit and press down on it with the tip of my tongue and then I move it side to side with my tongue, licking it and slurping up Kerry's juices. She tastes amazing, salty and sweet all at once and her taste and her scent consume me, pushing me closer to the edge myself as I become lost in Kerry. She envelopes me, taking over all of my senses and infiltrating them so that we become one.

I run my hands over her thighs as I lick her. I can hear her moaning and gasping as I work her. I keep licking, pressing down harder on her, getting her ready to go over the edge. I can feel her clit pulsing under my tongue and I know she's almost there. I move my tongue away from her clit and replace it with my fingers, working her hard and fast.

She's leaning back on her hands, her head thrown back and her back arched. She looks amazing as she takes the pleasure I give her. I get to my feet as my fingers work her and with my other hand, I pull her blouse out of her waist band and begin to unbutton it. When it's open, I lightly run my fingernails over her belly and chest. She sucks in a breath, pressing herself against my hand and I watch as her skin puckers and goosebumps chase each other over her skin.

I up the pace of my probing fingers and I know Kerry is almost there. Her face contorts and her muscles go rigid as pleasure assaults her. I keep rubbing her clit as her mouth opens and closes as she moans my name.

Finally, I move my fingers from her clit, but I don't give her any reprieve from her pleasure. I quickly unbutton my trousers and push them down over my thighs, my boxer shorts seconds behind them. I run my cock through Kerry's slit, spreading her wetness all around, feeling her sticky juices coating me, and then I plunge into her warm depths.

Her hot slippery flesh engulfs me, pulling me in deeper and I have to pause for a second to get myself back under a semblance of control before I begin to move inside of her, feeling the tight caress of her pussy. God, she feels amazing and I take a second to wonder how I got so lucky. It is only a second and then I am caught up in the moment again, any thoughts other than the thoughts of our bodies connecting as one are banished.

Kerry tightens around me, her pussy still contracting from the climax she reached seconds before I entered her, and I gasp as pleasure grips me, moving through my body and making me feel like I am floating on gentle caressing air. I put my hands on Kerry's hips and pull her against me, moving her in time with my thrusts, going deeper and deeper into her, filling her completely.

Kerry clenches her pussy around me again, intentionally this time, sending shockwaves of pleasure through my body and I know I can't hold myself back for much longer. I up my pace, thrusting into her hard and fast. She cries out and her pussy clenches again as another orgasm takes her. A rush of wetness leaves her, dousing me in her pleasure. The warmth of her juices on me pushes me over the edge and I know I have lost the battle to hold myself back this time.

I feel my own climax overtake me, my cock spasming and twitching inside of Kerry's pussy, and my whole body coming to life as each nerve ending is flooded with ecstasy. I still hold Kerry's hips, holding her in place against me as I spurt into her over and over again. I try to say her name, but I can't make my mouth and brain connect and instead of her name, all I manage is a strangled sounding grunt as I am held in the throes of pleasure.

Finally, my orgasm begins to fade and I slowly come back down to earth. I release Kerry's hips and tuck my hands beneath her waist instead. My cock slips out of her and I pull her into a sitting position. Her eyes have rolled back in her head, but they come back down and she blinks them into focus as I straighten her up. She gives me a lazy, sated looking smile.

"Wow," she breathes.

"Yeah that," I smile.

She leans against my chest and we wrap our arms around each other as we get ourselves back under control. I can feel Kerry's heart racing, her chest heaving as she pants for air, and I'm sure she can feel the same thing coming from me.

"I should tell you I'm pregnant more often," Kerry says after a moment, a touch of amusement in her voice.

I nod, laughing softly, and then I kiss the top of Kerry's head, breathing in the coconut scent of her hair, and squeeze her tightly to me. I still can't quite believe my luck. I'm going to be a dad, and I'm going to do it with Kerry by my side if she'll have me.

BLAKE

I can't keep the smile off my face as I head for the diner around the corner from the office. I'm meeting Kerry for lunch which obviously I am happy about anyway, but to be honest it's more than that; I haven't been able to stop smiling since the moment Kerry told me I was going to be a dad.

I've always wanted kids, but up until the moment Kerry announced I was about to have one, it had always been a sort of abstract want, like something that would happen in the future. But now it's real, and rather than scaring me, which I would have said it would have done if someone had asked me how I would have felt about this before I heard the news, it has left me feeling exhilarated and more excited for the future than I've ever been. I'm going to be a dad and I'm going to be the best dad I can be. I will do whatever it takes to make sure my son or daughter is happy and healthy and knows they are loved.

I reach the diner and see Kerry already seated in a booth. She gives me a wave as she spots me and I cross the floor and join her.

"I ordered you a burger and fries. I hope that's ok, but I was starving and I didn't want to wait," she says.

"I can't really complain even if I wanted to can I? Not now you can just say the baby wanted it," I smile.

"I'm glad you're seeing things my way," Kerry laughs.

I smile and squeeze her hand across the table.

"I'm not crazy enough to get on the wrong side of you now you're full of pregnancy hormones," I say.

Kerry laughs and shakes her head.

"I'm honestly not sure whether to be glad about that or to take it as an insult," she laughs.

"Take it as it was meant – as a joke. And let's get real here. I'm never going to be angry about someone getting me a burger and fries," I reply.

Kerry grins and then our food arrives and we start to eat it. My burger is lovely, juicy and tender, and Kerry says her chicken burger is good too. We eat in a comfortable silence for the most part, exchanging the odd observation about the food or something we hear on the radio that's playing in the background.

When we're done eating, I know it's time for me to ask Kerry if we can make things official between us. I am suddenly nervous, afraid that she'll say no and I will be stuck alone, without Kerry and left being a weekend dad. I wonder if I should maybe put off asking her, but I know that's not a good idea. The longer I leave it, the more nervous I will get. I have never been afraid to go after something I want before, and I want Kerry and our baby, our family, more than I've ever wanted anything. And now I have to be strong and just put that out there.

"I wanted to ask you something," I say.

"Ok, go on then," Kerry says, smiling encouragingly at me across the table.

She has the tiniest dab of tomato ketchup on her lip and I reach out and wipe it off with my thumb.

"Thanks," she says smiling sheepishly and blushing ever so slightly.

"Kerry, I know we haven't always seen eye to eye, but lately I think we have and now we're going to be parents. Together. And well, I really like you, and I wondered if you would maybe like to make this official. You know, for us to be exclusive," I say.

Kerry's smile widens.

"Are you asking me to be your girlfriend like we're twelve years old?" she grins.

"Yeah, I guess I am," I laugh.

I hadn't thought of it that way. It just felt right to ask her. She's laughing though and for all she's teasing me, I think she's probably as glad as I am that we've had this conversation. At least now we both know for sure where we stand instead of us both just hoping that we're exclusive.

"You know, maybe you should have asked me that before you knocked me up. Just a thought," Kerry says.

I feel my heart start to sink but then I see the sparkle of mischief in Kerry's eyes and the dimple in her cheek as she tries to stop herself from smiling.

"Yeah you're right. I missed my chance. Never mind, I've learned for the next one," I say.

I pretend to get up and leave and Kerry grabs my wrist and pulls me back down, both of us laughing.

"Yes," she says. "I'll be your girlfriend."

"Good," I smile.

It seems today is a day for Kerry to continue making me the happiest man on earth. First with her pregnancy news and now by agreeing to be my girlfriend. I know by the feeling I have inside of myself when Kerry says yes to being with me properly, officially, that this is serious for me now. I have fallen for Kerry and I have fallen for her hard. I don't tell her that. Not yet. I don't want her to think I'm coming on too strong. I'll let her come around to the idea of us being more than just a casual boyfriend and girlfriend in her own time.

It's funny how we got here. I still can't quite believe that the woman who annoyed me more than anyone I had ever met before has become the one woman who I can't bear to be without. If someone had told me I would be with Kerry and be happier than I've ever been before in these last few months, I would have told them that they were insane. And yet here I am in that exact situation.

I still don't know how things turned out so great between us, but it is what it is, and I am most certainly not complaining about it. I guess sometimes it doesn't really matter how you got there or why you were headed that way in the first place – all that matters is that you get there. And I have certainly done that.

KERRY

I sit in front of my computer in my office after my lunch with Blake. I am still glowing from him asking me to make our thing official. I teased him about asking me to be his girlfriend, but I'm also kind of pleased that he did it. It leaves no doubt that we're for real here.

I shake my head, trying to shake away thoughts of Blake and us being a thing and even of me being pregnant. I have to focus on work right now. I have just finished up the final part of the report Blake and I need for this afternoon's shareholder meeting.

I double check and then triple check all of the figures. After our last meeting, I am more than aware that everything needs to be perfect – hell it needs to be even better than perfect. The shareholders have given us a second chance after the fiasco with the figures the last time. If there are any mistakes this time, I fear we will ostracise them completely this time. If our shareholders pull out of their investments with us, Blake and my dad stand to lose the company and we have to make sure that doesn't happen. It would be heart-breaking to see that happen at the best of times, but to see it happen when we are onto something magical over a little mistake would be too much to bear.

I debate calling Blake and having him come by my office and go over the whole report with me, but that will make me look insecure and pathetic. I have checked the damned thing three times. I know it's right. I don't need Blake or anyone else to come and hold my hand and reassure me that I haven't just randomly forgotten how to do my job.

I shut down the report and make sure it's saved to my desktop so I can grab it easily when I need to link it up to the projector screen. I close my laptop and get up and pick it up along with my cell phone. I make my way to the conference room. I am half an hour early and after I set up the laptop on the projector, I pour myself a large coffee and sit down and start sipping it. As I sip it, I go over everything in my head, rehearsing what I will say and when. Just the key points. I don't want to sound like a robot, like my speech is rehearsed. I like to sound natural, like we're all just friends having a chat together in this kind of meeting.

I have never had a problem nailing that tone before, but I have to admit that the last meeting has thrown my confidence a little bit. Or truthfully, it's thrown my confidence a lot. I close my eyes and massage my temples. I take a deep breath, willing myself to calm down, telling myself it's going to be fine.

My laptop makes a pinging sound and I open my eyes with a frown. I shut down my browser before I sat down so that this sort of thing couldn't happen. I get up and go to my laptop, but my browser is indeed shut. Nothing is open. I frown. Did I imagine the electronic pinging sound?

I know I didn't. I'm not an idiot.

The door to the conference room opens and one of the shareholders comes in.

"I have to go. I'm just stepping into a meeting," he says into his cell phone.

I smile to myself, filled with relief. My laptop isn't going to have some sort of breakdown during my presentation and I'm not going crazy. The beeping sound must have come from the shareholders cell phone and I just heard it from the corridor.

"Good afternoon," I smile, extending my hand.

"Good afternoon," he replies, shaking it. "Am I early?"

He looks around at the empty room and raises an eyebrow.

"A little bit," I admit. "But it's fine. Would you like a drink while we wait for everyone else to get here?"

The rest of the time before the meeting flies in a whirl of greeting the other shareholders as they arrive and pouring drinks for them all. Somewhere in the midst of it all, Blake arrives and helps with the drinks orders. When everyone is here and all seated and settled with their refreshments, I glance at Blake and he nods encouragingly at me. I take a deep, calming breath and then I stand up and move to the head of the conference room table where my laptop is. I turn and smile around the room, meeting everyone's eye as I look them over.

"Thank you all for coming today," I start. "It's going to give me great pleasure to show you the profit margins we're working on. But I do believe it will give you guys even greater pleasure when you see the money you all stand to make from this development."

I am already starting to feel confident once more. As soon as I start talking it's like I slip into the old me, the me who would have stood up here and talked with no qualms whatsoever. I am glad to know that part of me still exists. It would have been ridiculous to let one little mistake knock my confidence completely.

"Before we dive right in, I would first like to take a moment to personally apologize to you all about the hiccup in the last meeting. Did everyone get their copy of the correct report?" I say.

I look around the table. The shareholders are mostly all nodding their heads. A couple of them just look back at me and I decide to take that as a yes. I'm sure they'd be making it known if they hadn't received the report.

"Good," I say with a curt nod and then I move on, starting my presentation and clicking through the slides.

I talk them through the plans for certain elements of the designs and how we are coming on with the building work and the high level of presales interest we've generated. They all seem pleased enough with what I'm telling them, and I really start to relax now. They seem happy already and I haven't even got to the good bit yet; the bit where I show them the bargain materials we managed to get hold of, and how it has increased our profit margin by almost twenty percent.

I am smiling as I click through to the financial report. The smile freezes on my face and then slowly begins to slip from it as I see the expressions on the faces before me. I turn to glance at the screen where the figures are being projected.

I can hardly believe what I am seeing. The figures are all wrong once again. No. No. No. This can't be happening again. It just can't be. I know those figures were right when I checked the report before I left my office. I know it. And yet now they are completely wrong. Mr. Andrews, who seems to have been voted as some sort of spokesman for the whole group of shareholders, clears his throat. I glance at him and he looks back at me, looking slightly uncomfortable.

"Kerry, let me stop you there while we go over these figures properly. I appreciate you trying to make us some extra money naturally, and I think it's safe to say we all feel the same on that score. But not like this," he says.

I know what he's thinking. The figures I am currently displaying make it look like I was telling the truth about the profit margins. But not about where savings were coming from. These reports make it look like we have over spent on several areas of the project and then panicked and tried to make the money back anyway we could. Including illegal ways. It looks like we have been laundering money through the company's books.

"Mr. Andrews, let me assure you that this is not even close to what it looks like," I say. "I wish I could explain what's happened, but right now, I can't. All I can say is that those are not the figures I put into my report."

"You mean to tell me the wrong figures are being presented to us again?" Mr. Andrews demands.

I nod. What else can I do? That's exactly what I'm having to tell him.

"Well I suppose that is preferable to the other alternative, but it's still not good enough. This is the second time we have been called in here and given the wrong information. It worries me. Because if you're doing this with us, what's to say you're all not giving clients the wrong information as well?" Mr. Andrews says.

"I assure you we're not," I say quickly hoping I can appease him a little bit. It doesn't work.

"But presumably you would have said the same thing about the information you're giving us being correct prior to this happening," he points out.

I look down at the ground, because once more, he is completely right. I have no idea what to say to make this better, and I am glad when I hear a chair scraping across the ground and see Blake standing up.

"Ok everyone, clearly there has been some sort of mistake here, and all we can do is apologize. I promise you all I will get to the bottom of this, and when I do, the appropriate action will be taken," Blake says. "Thank you all for your time today, and I will have the correct figures sent across to you as soon as I can."

There is a further scraping of chairs as the shareholders accept that they are being dismissed. They begin to file out of the room. I get a few sympathetic looks, but most of them just looked pissed off. A few even shake their heads at me. When the last of them has gone, I move to the conference room door and push it closed.

Now is the moment of truth. I am dreading turning around to face Blake. I know he apologized last time he went off on me, and I'm sure he'll be a bit nicer about telling me to pack up and go, but he's obviously going to think this is my mistake. I mean who else can he blame? I did the report. Still though, I have to at least try to make my case. If I don't, then of course he will think it's me. At this point, quiet acceptance is as good as a confession.

"I have no idea what happened there," I say. "But I do know those figures were right when I left my office. It sounds crazy and impossible, but it's the truth."

BLAKE

I don't even stop to think about it. As impossible as it sounds that the figures were right when Kerry checked the report in her office and now they're not, I believe her. I made the mistake of not believing her once, and I won't do that again. I know Kerry. She doesn't make mistakes like this, and I have never known her to lie to cover herself. She would own up if she'd fucked up. I don't know why I couldn't see any of that the first time this happened.

"I know," I say. "And we'll get to the bottom of it. Someone is out to sabotage this project and I intend to find out who it is and why they're doing it."

"You mean you believe me?" Kerry asks, looking at me in surprise. "You know I didn't fuck this up?"

"Of course I do," I say. "I only regret that I didn't handle the first time this happened better. I know you didn't do this."

She nods and I think for a moment.

"After you checked the figures for the last time in your office, did you go to the bathroom or to the staff room for a drink or anything?" I ask. "Was your laptop unattended at all?"

"No," Kerry says. "I checked everything for the third time and then I came here and got everything set up. That's why it sounds impossible. The laptop was never out of my sight. So unless someone invisible did it, then I honestly can't explain how it could have happened."

Knowing that the laptop was never left unattended after the report was finalised and checked does make things slightly more complicated. I was hoping Kerry had left her office for a moment and someone had slipped in.

"Hang on a minute. Could it... it might be possible. Ok, this might sound crazy. I'm not even sure if it is possible, but I think it is," Kerry says, suddenly looking excited. "But could the report have been changed remotely? Like does anyone but you and me have access to it? Because I swear that the laptop pinged like something had happened, but I went to investigate and nothing was open. One of the shareholders came in right after that and he was talking on his cell phone so I just assumed the noise was from that. But what if it wasn't? What if it was from the laptop, from changes being saved on our report?"

I consider what she's saying. That makes sense. In theory, only Kerry and I have access to the report, but someone else could have gotten into it. I don't know what would motivate someone to do that, but I'll find out. First, I have to work out who is responsible for this. And Kerry has given me a good starting point to get that information. I think for a moment.

"Can you get the right figures sent to the shareholders for me please? I'm going to go down to the IT department and try to figure out if someone else has been accessing the report," I say.

Kerry nods and stands up already heading for the door. She looks fired up now she has been given a task to do. She turns back to me before she opens the door and smiles at me.

"Thank you. For believing in me," she says.

She's gone before I can tell her that I will always believe in her, but I think, or at least I hope, that she knows that now.

~

I've been in IT for the better part of an hour and we are finally getting somewhere. Carl, the IT guy nods and smiles and then he turns to me.

"So at a quick glance, there is only yourself and Miss Morgan who have access to the document in question. However, there is a back door for want of a better word. A way for someone to access the report without leaving a trace of themselves in any of the obvious places," he says.

He pauses, waiting for me to catch up with his train of thinking. I nod for him to go on. I don't have an in-depth knowledge of technology like Carl does, but I know enough to know that he's saying someone could have hacked into the document.

"So see here?" Carl says, pointing at his screen. I look and see three numbers. I nod although I have no real clue what I'm looking at. "Those are IP addresses. Each computer or laptop here has a unique one. The top one is yours. The middle one is Miss Morgan's. And the last one is someone who has accessed this document who isn't either of you two."

"And we can find out who that is?" I say, hardly daring to believe we are on the verge of getting to the bottom of this.

Carl nods his head.

"Yes. Assuming they are using their company computer," he says.

He highlights the bottom IP address and copies it, and then he opens a new program and pastes it in. The program displays the little blue circle that means either something is happening or the damned thing has frozen. In this case, something is happening, because in seconds, I am given a name.

Annette Peterson. My heart sinks. There is no way that Annette did this. She's worked here for years and she's on Kerry's team. I sigh.

"Not who you wanted it to be?" Carl asks.

I shake my head.

"No – I don't have any idea who it might be to be honest. But I know it's not Annette. She's just not someone who would do this," I say.

Carl shrugs.

"It doesn't have to be her specifically. It was just her computer that was used to do it. I mean presumably she leaves the office for breaks and stuff. And maybe whoever is doing it realizes they can be traced and so used someone else's computer to further cover their tracks," he says.

I consider this and then I smile and clap Carl on the shoulder.

"You know what? You might be onto something there. Thanks Carl," I say.

I get up and head back out of IT. I go to Kerry's office and step inside.

"Did you get the real report sent out?" I ask.

Kerry looks up from her work and nods her head.

"Yeah. Did you find anything?" she asks.

I go to her desk and sit down.

"Yes and no," I say.

I quickly explain everything Carl told me and about Annette's name coming up and how someone must have used her computer.

"Or it was Annette herself," Kerry says.

"Well yes, I mean in theory that's possible. But does it seem likely to you that Annette would go into the report and tamper with it like that?" I ask.

Kerry shrugs her shoulders.

"Honestly, I would have said no a couple of months ago, but now I'm not so sure. Don't you think it's a little bit strange that Annette is involved in this either directly or indirectly and she was also the one who ended up taking over booking our hotel rooms for that conference? Remember, the rooms were booked wrong. We thought it was a mistake at the time, but what if it wasn't?" Kerry says.

I think for a moment. I guess she has a point, but there's something I still don't understand.

"Annette isn't working on this project, so if it turns out to be her who changed those figures, it wasn't a mistake, it was intentional. Can you think of any reason why she would want to sabotage the company she has worked at for so long?" I ask.

Kerry shakes her head.

"No. But what if that's not what this is about? What if she hasn't realized it's that serious. I think she might know about us somehow and is jealous. It feels like everything being done was meant to try and make you and I fight," she says.

"Ok, in theory, that makes sense. But Annette isn't into me," I point out. "So why would she be jealous." I pause and grin at Kerry. "Or do you think she's into you?"

"No, of course I don't think she's into me," Kerry says, shaking her head and rolling her eyes at me.

"So if she's not into either of us, then why would she be jealous if she knows we're together?" I press her.

"Well, what if maybe she is into you and she just hides it well," Kerry shrugs. "There's one way to find out. Let's go and confront her and see exactly what she has to say for herself."

I know I should really do that alone. It's not professional to have Kerry with me while I talk to Annette, but I know Kerry will take some talking out of this one, and to be fair, she is involved in this. It's her reputation on the line, perhaps even her job on the line if we can't prove that either Annette is behind this, or someone else used her computer. Besides, the way I see it is this; if Annette is guilty of trying to sabotage this project for whatever reason, then I really don't care if she's embarrassed to have Kerry present while I talk to her about it. And if she isn't guilty and her computer has just been used to sabotage the report, then I can't see any reason why she would object to speaking about the situation with Kerry present.

"Ok, let's do it," I say, hoping I have made the right decision.

Kerry stands up and starts for her office door. I stand up too and I put my hand on Kerry's arm, stopping her for a second. It's one thing to have her accompany me to Annette's office, but I can't have her running off with an accusation or anything like that. Kerry looks up at me with a questioning frown on her face.

"What? Don't say you've changed your mind," she says.

"No of course I haven't. Just when we get to Annette's office, let me do the talking ok?" I caution her.

Kerry nods her head but I have no idea whether she'll be able to keep her mouth shut if she suspects Annette is lying to us. I guess there's only one way to find out. It's not too late to call this off and tell Kerry to wait in her office, but the truth is, either Kerry or Annette are likely to be pissed off with me within the next ten minutes, and I would much rather it be Annette than Kerry.

That tells me everything I need to know about whether or not I'm going to go through with letting her accompany me. I release Kerry's arm and nod towards her office door and then I follow her from the office. We head along the hallway, pausing to speak to a few employees as they pass us by. We reach Annette's office door and I raise my hand and tap on the door and wait for her to answer.

"You own the company. You don't have to knock on anyone's office door," Kerry points out with an amused look on her face.

"I knock on your office door," I point out.

"Come in," Annette shouts from inside her office.

"Yeah but I'm not trying to sabotage the biggest project we've ever had," Kerry says, the look of amusement slipping from her face as my hand moves to Annette's door handle. I raise my eyebrows at Kerry and she lifts her hands in surrender. "Ok, ok, I'll be good. I promise."

I push the door open and Annette smiles up at me from behind her desk. Her smile slips slightly when she sees Kerry is with me. Is that a show of guilt or is she just confused as to why we're both rocking up at her office together? I guess that's what we're about to find out.

"Um, hi," Annette says, looking from me to Kerry and back again. "What's up?"

"We're just going around giving all of the staff a head's up," I say. "There was some issues with the figures for our latest project and our biggest shareholders are pulling out, so we're looking at layoffs in the next few weeks."

I say a silent prayer that it works. Annette looks down at her desk for a moment and then she looks back up at me. Her face is flushed red, her eyes too wide, and the expression gives away her guilt.

Come on, I think, spill it.

Annette blinks a couple of times and then she looks away from me again. She looks down into her lap and fiddles with

219

her skirt for a second and then she looks back up at me in an almost uncomprehending manner like she's forgotten why I am here. Her bottom lip quivers slightly and I know then that we've got her. It's not that she doesn't comprehend what's going on; it's more that she doesn't comprehend how we got here to this moment.

"You don't have to do that," Annette says. "Don't lay anyone off. Tell the shareholders the truth; the inconsistencies on the reports were my fault."

I cheer inside. I didn't even dare to hope that Annette would have a total rush of conscience and confess openly. I just need to get her to say a bit more and then we can deal with this properly. At the moment, she hasn't said enough to imply it's not just a mistake on her part, and while I know it's more than that by her reaction, our HR department will need more than that to go on to make any punishment I dole out stick and keep us within the law at the same time.

KERRY

It took me a moment or two to realize what Blake was doing when he told Annette about layoffs. I can't believe I didn't work it out sooner. I'm just glad Annette didn't either. I have to admit that I was shocked when she just admitted it. I mean she obviously didn't have much of a conscience when she was putting the project at risk with her tampering, so why now?

"Why did you change the figures Annette?" Blake asks her gently. "What were you trying to achieve?"

"I did it because it was the only way I could think of to get rid of her," Annette says, pointing at me.

I feel my jaw drop open and Blake looks as shocked as I feel.

"What? Why would you want to get rid of me, Annette? I thought we were friends," I blurt out.

I know Blake told me to let him do the talking, but this is too much to take in without me being able to ask any questions. Now Annette has admitted she did it to get rid of me, Blake will surely understand why I had to speak up. It's so much worse than her liking Blake and being jealous. This makes it personal.

"You took my job," Annette says bitterly. "I came to this company with the implied promise of a promotion if I performed. And I did perform, I know I did. But the boss's daughter was always going to get ahead of me right? I figured if you got told to leave, I'd get the job I actually deserve."

I open my mouth again, though I don't quite know what to say to that. I can't believe Annette seriously thinks I only got my promotion because of who my dad is. She obviously doesn't know the first thing about my dad – he would never risk the company going downhill because he put the wrong person into a role. I got the promotion because I deserved it and because I out performed Annette on every bit of criteria for the manager's job. My sales figures were always better than hers and my clients were always higher end and that's just the start of it.

I debate between explaining this to her, or yelling at her to mind her own fucking business and not mess with me. In the end, I close my mouth and I do neither – I just can't find the right words to say anything right now. I feel like I should be angry with Annette, but now that she's come clean, I've surprised myself. I'm not that angry really. I just feel sorry for her. Like the whole thing is kind of pathetic when you think about it.

Blake seems to regain his composure quicker than I do and he shakes his head sadly. Unlike me, he doesn't seem to struggle to find the words he wants to say.

"Well Annette you're going to get exactly what you deserve from this company right now. You're fired. Please collect your things and leave immediately," he says, his voice quiet, almost gentle.

Annette nods her head, looking equally sad but not surprised at the news that she's fired. She pulls open the top drawer of her desk and takes out her handbag and then she picks up a photo from her desk.

"That's it," she says. "Everything else belongs to the company."

Blake nods his head.

"I'll escort you to the parking lot, unless you'd prefer to have security do it," he says.

Annette shakes her head.

"No, you don't need to call them. I'll go quietly. I guess your reaction to this has made me realize I will never advance at this company and it's better for us all if I just go now," she says.

Blake nods his head.

"I'm inclined to agree with that. Your final paycheck will be forwarded on to you," he says.

I watch as Blake leads Annette from the room. She doesn't so much as glance back at me. Once they are out of sight, I sit down at Annette's old desk and run my hands over my face. I can't believe Annette would try to get me fired like that, but really, the strongest thing I feel right now is relief that it is over. Maybe now we'll be able to get through a presentation with all of the right information on display.

EPILOGUE

KERRY

One Year Later

I smile at Blake across the table. He smiles back and raises his glass of Diet Coke into the air.

"I know it's not exactly champagne, but I wanted to propose a toast all the same. To us and to the successful completion of the development," he says.

I smile at him and raise my own glass of iced tea.

"To us and to the development," I repeat.

We clink our glasses together and sip our drinks, and then we put our glasses back down as our waiter appears with our meals. He places them down and we thank him and then we begin to eat our pasta as he moves away. I have only eaten two forkfuls when I check my watch. Blake catches me and laughs.

"Will you relax," he says. "We've barely been out for half an hour and we told the babysitter we'd be out for two or three hours."

"I know," I sigh. "I'm just a bit nervous that's all. Leaving Maya alone for the first time is scary."

"She's not alone, she's with the babysitter. Now eat and relax and stop worrying," Blake laughs. "She's not due a feed and she was already down for the night when we left the house."

"Ok, distract me," I say.

"What here?" Blake says, looking around. "Well if you say so."

His hand moves towards the zipper on his jeans and I laugh and shake my head.

"I didn't mean that," I say, still laughing.

"It worked though didn't it," Blake winks. "It got you laughing."

I have to admit he's right about that.

"It feels good to laugh," I say. "And it feels really good not to have anything hanging over our heads again."

"Tell me about it," Blake says. "It was touch and go for a while with the shareholders?"

"Yeah. Thank goodness enough of them understand finance to realize that it was equally likely we'd been set up than that we'd been money laundering and when everything else came together, it pretty much convinced them all," I agree. "I knew it was going to take a while to convince them we were clean, but I didn't expect it to take all year."

"I still can't believe we pulled it off, with or without Annette meddling. It's the most profitable development the company has ever worked on," Blake says.

"What do you expect with the A team working on it," I laugh.

"Fair point," Blake agrees with a grin. His grin fades and he takes my hand across the table. "I'm so sorry I doubted you at the beginning of the project."

"Oh forget about it, it's water under the bridge. You've already apologized for that and it's forgotten now ok?" I say.

He smiles and nods his head.

"I just wanted you to hear that I was sorry one more time," he says.

"Well that's the last time I want to hear it," I say.

"You're amazing," Blake grins. "I love you all the world and back again."

"Now that I want to hear all the time," I grin. "You can say that as often as you like."

"I love you, I love you, I love you," Blake grins.

"I love you too," I giggle.

"Maybe that's why we're the A team," Blake says. "You know because we're all loved up and shit."

I roll my eyes at his turn of phrase and then I consider his idea.

"I don't know about that," I say, chewing thoughtfully. "I mean we were pretty damned good even when we hated each other."

I smile and Blake smiles back at me.

"Can you believe how much things have changed between us?" he says.

"Not at all," I reply. "It's crazy how things turn out isn't it?"

"It is. Do you ever worry that we'll switch over again and go back to hating each other?" Blake says.

I shake my head and laugh.

"No. Not even a little bit. Why, do you?" I say.

Blake shakes his head.

"No. In fact I think we should agree right now to work on all of the big projects together," he says.

"Deal," I agree immediately.

He reaches down into his pocket with one hand and smiles at me again.

"Including this big project they call life," he says. He pulls his hand from his pocket and he's holding a small, red velvet box which he opens to show me a beautiful diamond ring. I gasp when I see it. "Kerry, I love you now and forever. Will you marry me?"

"Yes," I say, tears filling my eyes. "Oh my God, yes."

Blake pushes the ring onto my finger and then he jumps up and comes around to my side of the table. He kisses me hard on the mouth and I let him, not caring even a little bit that we are in a public place. In the moment, it's like Blake and I are the only two people in the whole world, and that's just the way I like it. Me, Blake and Maya forever in our own little happy bubble.

The End

COMING SOON..

TROUBLE WITH THE CEO

Chapter One
Ava

"Shots, shots, shots, shots," Sophie chants, looking down at the shots before looking up at me expectantly, a massive grin on her face that says she knows I'm going to protest but that she also knows she'll be able to wear me down.

I glance down at the tray loaded with Sambuca shots in a range of colors that span the rainbow. I groan and shake my head. She's not going to be able to wear me down this time. I can't drink another shot. Even the thought makes me want to retch.

"No more for me," I say, holding my hands up and shaking my head vigorously. "I'm done here."

"Oh, come on Ava, don't be boring. We're meant to be celebrating graduating from university," Melanie adds, pushing one of the shots towards me with great determination.

I watch it slide towards me with a look of horror.

Melanie just laughs and keeps pushing the glass.

"Drink it, or it'll spill and what a waste that will be," she chants.

I shake my head.

"This is a once in a lifetime celebration," she cajoles.

"Do want me to be sick?"

"You're not going to be sick. Anyway, it's not a celebration if you don't wake up with a hangover."

I stare at her.

"Come on. Don't let me get drunk on my own." She pushes her lip out like a pouty child." Please, Ava, please."

"Ok, Ok," I laugh, holding my hands up in mock surrender.

Melanie stops pushing the little glass but her hand hovers around, ready to start up again if I back out now.

"But I swear this one is my last one."

I know I should have stood my ground, but Melanie is right. We're meant to be celebrating and it's not like we graduate university every day. Ah fuck it. I'm only going to do this once so I may as well make it a good one I tell myself.

"Sure, that's your last shot," Sophie agrees with a wink that says 'until the next one'. "Now drink up."

I shake my head and roll my eyes, but I can't help but smile as I pick my shot up and down it. It burns my throat as I swallow it and my mouth floods with saliva at the aniseed taste. It's mixed with banana flavor, not a good combination in any way, and the taste of the aniseed mingled in with the fake sweetness of the banana makes me want to retch once more, and I quickly swallow a mouthful of my gin and lemonade to swill away the taste. Sophie and Melanie look as though they enjoyed their shots about as much as I did.

"Remind me again why we drink these things when none of us actually like them," I ask, still grimacing from the sickly taste of the shot.

"Because they hit the spot." Melanie laughs, rubbing her belly.

I laugh with her. She kind of has a point. Once I get past the urge to retch, the warm feeling spreading through me is kind of nice. I am already floating on air after graduating from university and the shots only make me feel even more giddy, even more happy.

Sophie grins at me and holds out another shot to me. I shake my head but Sophie makes no effort to take the shot away.

"Two for you because you're celebrating two things," she says. "Graduating and getting the job you wanted."

"It's kind of the same thing really," I say. "I already had the job offer dependent on me graduating."

"Irrelevant. You still need to celebrate," Sophie insists.

The last few shots must be doing their job because I no longer want to be sensible and refuse to drink the shot. Instead, I reach out, take it from Sophie and down it in one. I chase it down with a gulp of gin and tonic, then stand up.

"Come on girls, let's hit the dance floor," I shout above the music. "I love this freaking song."

We make our way across the club, pushing our way through the warm and writhing bodies until we find a space on the dance floor. Then we begin to move. The combination of the heat, the alcohol and the thrumming of the music makes me feel wild and untamed, like I can really let my hair down tonight and just have fun.

As the three of us dance and drink, I realize that I don't want this night to end. It feels good to have this one weekend where I am no longer a student and I'm not at work until Monday. It's one last weekend of freedom where nothing defines me and I am free to do whatever the hell I like. No studying to do, no assignments, no panicking about exams, and no work over the weekend. I love that. Even knowing it won't last forever doesn't make me sad like it perhaps should. In fact, I think knowing that it can't last forever is part of what makes it so special.

As I down the last of my drink, I', aware I'm more than a little bit tipsy now. But I don't care. It's not like I'm falling all over drunk. Not yet anyway. I am just at that pleasant stage of drunk where everything is funny, and all of my inhibitions are starting to fall away. It's also that level of drunk where I know if I stop drinking now, it will wear off quickly and I won't be able to get it back. With that thought in mind, I stop dancing.

"Are you ok?" Sophie yells over the music, looking at me with a frown of concern as I look for a way through the throng of bodies on the dance floor.

"Yeah," I shout. "I'm fine. Better than fine. Great in fact. I'm just going to the bar. Same again?"

Sophie and Melanie both nod and keep dancing and I finally spot a small opening in the crowd and I make my way through it to the bar. I order our drinks – another gin and tonic for me and two vodka and cokes for Melanie and Sophie - and then I take a moment to have a look around the club. The club is busy – busier than it was when we moved onto the dance floor - but it's not packed to the point where you can't move or where you can't get a drink without waiting for twenty minutes.

I get our drinks and pay for them and make my way back to Sophie and Melanie, somehow making it across the dance floor without spilling a drop. I hand the girls their drinks and start dancing again, taking a long drink of my gin and tonic. I kind of miss the burning heat of the shots and I wonder absently if I should have gotten more of them. No I think, that would have been a bad idea.

"Isn't that Darlene over there?" Melanie asks.

I look over at the area she's pointing to and I see that it is indeed Darlene. Great. Just the person I don't want to see tonight. Or any night really. It's not so much that Darlene and I are enemies, or even that we don't like each other as such, it's just that we're not each other's cup of tea. We're total opposites to each other and not in a good way.

I generally tend to be fairly quiet, and Darlene is pretty much the life of the party, and where I am happy to be a part of the group, Darlene has to always be the center of attention. I find her particular brand of obsessive attention seeking annoying and she probably finds me boring. She's kind of treated her time at the university as one long, four-year party and tonight, on the night to end it all it's no surprise that she's dressed to kill.

In a skin tight red body con dress and heels so high it would give me vertigo. If she fall, I would be surprised if she doesn't break her ankle. Still it probably wouldn't faze her – after all, it would get her some more attention.

I catch myself being a mean and I tell myself to stop it. It's likely the last time I will have to see her, and the last time she will make me feel boring and inferior. Ok, so there's a bit of truth. I always feel like Darlene is looking down at me – boring plain little Ava - and that when she does it, other people follow her lead.

"Hi girls," Darlene calls, waving manically as she spots us.

She starts making her way over to us, smiling as though we're all best friends. She must be drunk I think to myself, or she would know that she thinks I'm not up to her class. She reaches us, making walking in her sky scraper shoes look easy. She grabs me by my upper arms, and quickly air kisses each of my cheeks. Wow I really must have drunk too much because I feel quite shell-shocked when she releases me. She moves on to Sophie and Melanie. At least they saw what was coming and had a moment to prepare themselves.

"It's so good to see you all," she trills, her voice, as always, just a little bit too loud and that's saying something in a club. "I was so worried I wouldn't get to say goodbye to you'all. I mean I know we were hardly best friends, but four years is a long time to be around the same people, isn't it, and I reckon we'll all miss each other in our own little ways."

I would argue the point. I don't think I'll miss Darlene for one minute but I have to admit she makes a fair point about the people around us becoming familiar, and her sentiment is nicer than I would have ever have given her credit for. I nod and smile.

"Yeah. It was nice meeting you Darlene," I say.

"You too honey," she replies with a flash of her Hollywood white teeth.

She clearly doesn't know my name and normally the fake show of friendship would annoy me, but tonight I let it wash over me. So what if she doesn't know my name? I only know hers because she's such a drama queen. I can't exactly judge her for not making the time to get to know anything about me.

She starts talking just loud enough to catch the attention of the people around us, laughing even louder than that. People are glancing over, some in amusement, some rolling their eyes. And of course, a lot drooling over her. I can feel my face burning as the attention centers on our little group and I have to admit I'm more than relieved when Darlene moves on to the next unsuspecting group who she greets initially with a loud shriek across the club and a wave.

"You know," Sophie laughs when Darlene is out of ear shot. "I can never decide if I want to be more like Darlene, or if I want to be strive to be the opposite of her as much as I possibly can."

I kind of know what she means and I nod and laugh. For all Darlene is annoying at times, there is no denying that she always seems to be having fun and she always has a gaggle of interesting people around her. I think it would be nice to be so unashamedly who I am and have that confidence.

"I'd settle for being able to walk in shoes like that," Melanie puts in, getting back enthusiastic nods from both Sophie and I.

We go back to dancing and I soon realize my drink is empty once more. I wiggle my glass in the air.

"Whose round is it?" I ask.

"Yours," both Sophie and Melanie say together.

They look at each other and laugh and I shake my head.

"I got these," I remind them.

"Yeah, but some of us have tuition to pay," Sophie grins.

"Not to mention accommodation, food, bills, bills and more stupid bills to pay," Melanie adds. "Oh, and did I mention paying bills?"

"I have bills to pay," I remind her with a laugh. "And rent to cover. And believe it or not, no one gives me free food either."

"Well yeah, but you have a job that covers all of that stuff easily," Sophie says. "There's no way waiting tables, or working in a store, or something covers it all. That's why we all have a shit ton of student debt and you don't."

I suppose she has a point there. Mr. Kramer, my employer at Kramer and Foley, the law firm I work at, paid for me to go to university and get a law qualification. While a student, I worked part time but he still paid me my full salary, telling me that getting the degree was essentially part of the job.

I work as Mr. Kramer's legal secretary. I started as a general secretary when I left school and after a few months, Mr. Kramer asked me to be his personal secretary when his old one retired. After two years, he decided that he needed someone who understood the legal system a whole lot more than I did. I remember when he called me into his office and told me that. I thought I was being fired and I was so upset it took me a while to register the fact that not only was he not firing me, but the offer he was making me was more than I ever could have dreamed was possible.

I think now of my gorgeous uptown apartment that no student would ever be able to afford and my almost new, not cheap car, and I decide that yes, I can get another round in. I grin at the girls.

"Fine," I say, holding my hands up in surrender. "Same again?"

They both nod and I head back to the bar. The club is picking up now and the crowd is a little bit thicker but it's still not so bad that it's a tight squeeze at the bar. I order our drinks and pay for them. As I walk away from the bar, I spot Darlene again. She's heading towards the exit of the club with a guy hanging off her arm and most likely hanging on her every word while he's about it.

As they reach the door, she turns back to wave to someone and he turns around too and I see his face. He's damned hot. Darlene is clearly going home with him tonight. For the first time in my life I feel a pang of jealousy go through me at the thought of the night she is going to have. Horrified with myself I look away from them quickly and catch the eye of the waitress who is patrolling around the club selling shots from a tray. She raises the tray and an eyebrow in question and I nod my answer.

I move to the side slightly and put my drinks down on an empty table and fish some money out of my purse.

"Two please," I say.

"Seven dollars," the shot girl says.

I pay her and I am rewarded with two electric blue shots. I shrug and pick up the first one and down it. The second one follows soon after it. It's slightly better than the Sambuca shots, but not by much. As I pick up our drinks and then start to head back to the dance floor again, I know that Darlene had the right idea getting out of here with her hottie in tow. And in that moment, I know I am going to do the same thing tonight.

I am going to embrace my inner Darlene and have a fun night with a guy I have known for all of ten minutes and I'm going to enjoy it. I am going to let my hair down and have wild sex, the kind of sex I've only ever dreamed of having. But I am going to do one thing better than Darlene. The guy I go home with is going to be even hotter than hers. I smile to myself. Yes, that sounds like a damned good plan, even if I do say so myself.

I re-join the girls and by the time we finish our drinks and get some more, I have not forgotten my plan exactly, but I have convinced myself I was just being silly, just being drunk so to speak. I am no Darlene, nor do I want to be anything like her.

Still when I look up and spot the most handsome man I have ever seen in my life across the crowded room, I feel a stirring inside of myself, like my inner Darlene is waking up and giving me confidence.

"Go get him," she seems to say. "God Ava, have a one night where you just act your age and have fun."

That voice makes it sound so easy, and suddenly I see that it is that easy. I just need to act like I'm confident and the hot guy won't know that it's all a front. How could he? He doesn't know anything about me. I can be anyone I want to be while I am with him.

Suddenly the hot guy looks over towards me and for a split second, everything else fades away. I can't hear the pounding music anymore. I can't see the other people around me. All I can see is him.

And my God is he a sight to behold.

He's tall, a little bit over six foot I'd guess, and he has the sort of build that says he works out, but that he's not obsessed with building huge muscles. His dark brown hair is just long enough to hang in his eyes or get tosses about in the wind. He runs his fingers thought i as he looks at me.

I can feel my body responding to him as surely as if he was right by my side touching me. Goose bumps skitter back and forth across my skin and my clit tingles, my pussy dampening and longing to be filled by the handsome stranger.

The spell is broken when Sophie touches my shoulder. I half jump and look towards her. She frowns slightly.

"Are you ok?" she asks.

"Yeah, I'm fine. I was just lost in thought for a minute there," I say.

"Melanie needs to get out of here," Sophie says, nodding her head towards Melanie who stands beside her swaying wildly.

The drink seems to have hit Melanie all of a sudden and I think it's only Sophie's arm around her waist that is keeping her from falling over.

"I'm going to take her outside and grab a cab. Are you coming?" Sophie asks.

I start to nod, but I imagine the handsome stranger. I imagine that I can feel his warm lips on mine, his hands roaming over my body, and suddenly I am shaking my head.

"No. If you don't mind, I think I'm going to hang around and grab another drink or two," I say.

"Are you sure?" Sophie says, looking around herself dubiously as if she suddenly expects a group of armed ninjas to appear or something. "You want to stay here on your own?"

"A couple of old school friends are here. I promised I'd go and grab a drink and a catch up with them," I lie.

I don't know why I am lying. I could tell Sophie the truth, but something stops me and I don't question it, I just roll with it. This way will definitely invite less questions and I reckon that's a good thing.

"Well if you're definitely sure you'll be ok," Sophie says, her voice trailing off.

I am definitely sure I'll be ok, hell I'll be better than just ok if I get my way tonight, but Sophie is sounding less and less sure of the idea of me staying behind here alone by the minute. I am almost pleased when Melanie groans. She rubs her stomach with one hand and presses the other one to her mouth.

"Soph? I think I'm going to be sick," she says.

"Go," I tell Sophie who says a quick goodbye and starts to lead a very unsteady on her feet Melanie towards the exit.

They get through it without Melanie being sick which is a good thing. I feel kind of relieved once they're gone. I don't think I would have found the confidence to approach the handsome stranger with Melanie and Sophie watching me. But now there is nothing to stop me. If he rejects me, no one ever needs to know, so I have nothing to lose. But even as I think it, I know he won't reject me.

I know he should – he's at least three or four levels too hot for me – but I know he won't. I could see my own desire mirrored in his grey blue eyes when he looked at me. And I know it's only a matter of time before I am in his bed tonight.

Chapter Two
Christian

To say I'm not into clubbing would be an understatement. There was a time when I quite enjoyed it, when I was in my early twenties, but now, at thirty-one, I'm kind of over it. Yet here I am, standing in a club, the music pounding through me and the beer warming my insides nicely.

I usually can't stand the fact that the music is so loud that to talk to anyone you practically have to yell into their ear, but tonight, I am glad of the thumping sound of the bass going through me. It penetrates my brain and stops me from thinking. Because if I let myself think too much, all I am going to think about is my mom and the fact she has just been diagnosed with cancer. We don't know for sure how bad it is yet. It's in her breast, we know that much, but we don't know if it's spread anywhere else yet. Her oncologist has given her good odds if we've caught it early enough, but if we haven't and it's spread, then ...

No. I won't go there. I won't let myself think about the what ifs. Not tonight. No, tonight I will just keep the thumping sound in my mind, and if I really need to think, I'll think about that gorgeous red head I am taking home tonight. She's a far better distraction than any music could ever be no matter how loud the dj turned it up.

It was an accident that I spotted the gorgeous red head really. The club isn't exactly packed, but it's pretty full. Full enough that scanning your eyes around the room shouldn't be enough to really notice any one person over the others. But I noticed her alright.

It was her hair I noticed first – fire engine red, stick straight, and long enough to skim the tops of her breasts and draw the eye to them. It's the sort of hair that looks tacky on some girls, but not on this girl. On her it looked amazing, like she had been born to wear that color.

As I had watched her, she'd looked up and our eyes had met for a moment. It felt like we communicated without words in that moment, like she was telling me to take her home that night. I felt aroused just looking at her and my cock ached to feel her tight little pussy wrapped around it.

I could have approached her then, asked her if she wanted a drink. Or more. And I know she would have said yes to either. I could see it in her eyes, eyes that told me I was hers tonight. Sparkling, confident eyes. I thought about going over to her, but I couldn't take my eyes off her for long enough to make a move. I just wanted to keep staring at her, drinking her in. I could have sat there like that all night, but then one of the other girls with her touched her arm and spoke to her and she looked away and the spell was broken.

Only in that moment though. I know that neither of us will be leaving this club alone tonight. Maybe it would be more accurate to say the spell was paused for a moment or two.

I go to the bar and order a Jack Daniels and coke which I pay for and then I return to the place I was before. If the hot girl comes looking for me, that's where she'll look and I'd hate for us to accidentally miss each other. I don't know why I'm saying if she comes looking for me. I have never been more sure of anything in my life than I am about her. The way she looked at me was like she was already stripping me naked, already throwing me onto my back and straddling me. Yes, it's not if she comes looking for me. It's more when she comes looking for me.

I am almost finished my drink when I feel eyes on me. Instantly my skin tingles as though electric is buzzing over me. I know without looking up that it's her, but I look up anyway. How can I not look up? How can I not want to look into those pale green eyes again and lose myself in them once more?

I look up and of course I am right and it is her. And she's not just watching me this time. No, this time, she's walking towards me, her stride long and purposeful, her hips swaying seductively with each step. She is watching me and as I glance up and meet her eye, she smiles briefly, more a curling of the corners of her lips than anything. She looks down, runs her tongue over her bottom lip and then looks back up at me. I can hardly tear my eyes away from the glistening moisture her tongue leaves behind on her bottom lip. I ache to taste her, to hold her, to fuck her senseless.

I smile at her as she reaches me. She stops in front of me, looking up at me. I can't help but look down at her chest where her breasts move slightly with each breath she takes, her dress showing just the right amount of cleavage to be attractive while still being classy.

I look back up to her eyes - a sure sign of how gorgeous she is that my gaze is so easily drawn away from her body back to her eyes - and I bring my glass to my lips and drain the last of my drink, looking at her over the rim of the glass. I swallow and put the glass down, all without breaking eye contact with the gorgeous woman.

"Ready to leave?" I ask.

Want to read more?
Preorder here:
Trouble With The CEO

ABOUT THE AUTHOR

Thank you so much for reading!
If you have enjoyed the book and would like to leave a
precious review for me, please kindly do so here.

Tempted By The CEO

Please click on the link below to receive info about my latest
releases and giveaways.
NEVER MISS A THING

Or
come and say hello here:

ALSO BY IONA ROSE

Nanny Wanted

CEO's Secret Baby

New Boss, Old Enemy

Craving The CEO

Forbidden Touch

Crushing On My Doctor

Reckless Entanglement

Untangle My Heart

Tangled With The CEO

Tempted By The CEO